Watermelon Days & Firefly Nights

Center Point Large Print

**This Large Print Book carries the
Seal of Approval of N.A.V.H.**

Watermelon Days & Firefly Nights

HEARTWARMING SCENES FROM SMALL TOWN LIFE

Annette Smith

CENTER POINT LARGE PRINT
THORNDIKE, MAINE

Library of Congress Cataloging-in-Publication Data

Smith, Annette Gail, 1959–
[Short stories. Selections]
Watermelon days & Firefly nights : heartwarming scenes from small town life / Annette Smith. — Large Print Edition.
pages cm.
Summary: "A collection of heartwarming short stories set in a small town in Texas"—Provided by publisher.
ISBN 978-1-62899-204-5 (library binding : alk. paper)
1. Texas—Social life and customs—Fiction.
2. City and town life—Fiction. 3. Humorous stories, American.
4. Large type books. I. Title.
II. Title: Watermelon days and Firefly nights.
PS3619.M55W37 2014
813'.6—dc23
2014015782

To my four sisters-in-love.
In order of appearance,
Diana, Martha, Dale, and Sara.

Contents

Acknowledgments 9
Introduction 11

1. A Woman and a Well 15
2. Hot Dog's on the House 28
3. Let Her Eat Cake 38
4. Magic Money 57
5. Spanish Lessons 66
6. Angel Incognito 85
7. Millard and Millie 105
8. Blind Man's Bluff 118
9. Pinkie and the Chief 130
10. Scared Crow 148
11. Wise Woman 159
12. Butter Up 171
13. A Pinch of Sugar 191
14. Sweet Georgia 209
15. Old Spice 226
16. All the Right Ingredients 239

Acknowledgments

Thanks to the following folks:

My husband, Randy, for his willingness to subsist for days at a time on freezer food, his promises not to take his sweater off in public (thus revealing an unironed shirt), and his amazing ability to juggle the bills when the royalty check doesn't come, which makes it possible for me to live my dream of writing full time. He's simply the best.

My teenage daughter, Rachel, and my grown-up son, Russell, for convincing me of my worth and value, even when I'm not the mother I want to be.

Louie and Marolyn Woodall, my globe-trotting parents, for inspiring me to live a life of risk and adventure.

Dayne Woodall, my engineer brother, for the hours and hours he spends patiently walking me through my latest computer snafu.

Revell editor Lonnie Hull DuPont, for her encouragement and enthusiasm for my work and for making my writing fingers feel like they could fly.

Chip MacGregor, my agent and friend, for his expertise and guidance that helps keep me on track.

Special friends who, during the writing of this book, gave special support: Suzie Duke, Laura Jensen Walker, Sheila Cook, and Sheri Harrison.

To God be the glory!

Introduction

Ella Louise, Texas

Once the site of bustling activity, the outskirts of Ella Louise, Texas, where the railroad tracks once ran, now lie abandoned, given back over to the forest and overgrown with native pine trees, thick underbrush, noxious weeds, and snaky wild-berry vines. It's been forty years since the train stopped coming through Ella Louise. Rail routes changed, and with them a way of life.

Back then, most of Ella Louise's able-bodied men made their livings working in the woods, harvesting timber. Hauling cut trees to one of the town's two sawmills for processing, these men received a fair wage. With that wage, they supported their families. Problem was, both sawmills relied on the train to transport their products. When the train stopped coming to Ella Louise, the mills were forced to shut down.

The closing of the sawmills precipitated the dominolike flattening of Ella Louise's economy. The families of the mill workers packed up and left Ella Louise in droves. Lacking paying customers, most downtown businesses closed, one by one. The population of the town, which once hovered close to twelve thousand, dropped to near what it is today, just over twelve hundred.

To the average hiker, the woods where the railroad tracks once ran appear quiet and still. But superstitious old-timers swear up and down that if a person goes to the tracks and finds the right spot, he'll hear the whistle, the bell, and the clankety-clank sounds made by those long-gone trains. Nostalgic storytellers explain that since so many trains, making so much noise, passed through Ella Louise during its glory years, the sound of them remains in the woods. Although the sound is muffled beneath five decades of fallen pine straw and musty wild moss, on occasion it can be heard.

On at least a dozen occasions, I've traveled to Ella Louise, trekked to the site of the old railroad tracks, parked myself on a flat tree stump, and sat still and quiet as a doe, listening for the train.

I've yet to hear it.

Honestly? About an hour or so of listening is all I'm good for. After that, the bugs get to worrying me and my behind gets tired of its woody perch.

Kindly town folks who know about my quest express their regrets and ask if I'm disappointed by not hearing anything. Truthfully, I tell them, "Not much." For though the whistle of a phantom train would be something to hear, the sounds of life in present day, small-town Ella Louise are what I *really* come for.

I am a collector of stories, and in this small Texas town are tucked some of the most intriguing tales I've ever heard. I can't imagine that the sound of any train could compare with the rich collection of stories and yarns I've gleaned from Ella Louise's always friendly and flawed, often funny and eccentric population.

As you read the tales I've recorded in this book—many of them laugh-till-you-snort funny, a few of them touched with as much beauty and melancholy as a mourning dove's lonely dusk call—I trust that you, dear reader, will agree. So settle yourself in. Find a comfortable place to sit. Prop up your feet and fix yourself something good to drink. It's time you and I took a trip to the town of my dreams—Ella Louise.

1

A Woman and a Well

"*Okra* Festival? You sure?"

"Says right here." Nineteen-year-old newlywed Rochelle Shartle sat cross-legged in the rumpled bed, eating Little Debbie oatmeal cream pies and reading the newspaper to her groggy husband, Rocky. "The town of Ella Louise, Texas, invites all its friends and neighbors to attend this year's annual Okra Festival and Quilt Show."

"You like okra?" Rocky asked.

"Not really, but admission's free and there's a craft show and live music. It doesn't say anywhere that you have to eat okra. Come on. I want to do something today. It might be fun."

"I don't think so." Rocky had a project due for school that would take him all weekend to finish.

"How far is Ella Louise, anyway?" Rochelle asked, as if she hadn't heard him.

Rocky gave in after successfully extorting from Rochelle the promise that they would not stay too late.

The festival turned out to be a big deal, but even though they were only two amongst a small throng of visitors, Rocky and Rochelle found themselves personally greeted by the town's mayor, Alfred Tinker, who stood at the entrance of the festival grounds. As they walked past, Mayor Tinker handed them plastic okra-shaped lapel pins. Treated to all that the festival had to offer, they were spritzed with free Avon cologne—a brand-new scent—guided through the craft-show tent by two members of the Gentle Thimble Quilting Club, and pressed to sample fresh okra cooked seven different ways. ("Just spit it in your napkin when no one's looking," Rochelle whispered to Rocky when he looked about to gag.) In addition to the okra, there was a quilt raffle, a donkey softball game, and a nurse offering free blood-pressure checks.

"Leaving already?" asked the mayor, who was waving good-bye to people as they left the festival. "Come back and visit us real soon. Folks, did anyone tell you about the womanless wedding over at the Baptist church tonight? No, no. Not a *real* wedding. Fund-raiser. Town's trying to raise money for the volunteer fire department. They're needing a new truck. Sure y'all can't stay? It's sure to be an enjoyable evening, and we'd love to have you."

Rocky nixed the womanless wedding but let Rochelle talk him into driving around Ella

Louise and its outskirts before heading home.

A lot of work had gone into the preparation for the festival. Teens from the Methodist church youth group had done a trash pickup, and members of the Golden Spade Garden Club had placed whiskey-barrel halves planted with moss rose and red petunias all around the town square.

"Pretty," said Rochelle as they circled. "You think it's always this nice?"

"Looks like."

"Yards are full of flowers. Look at those daylilies—and those roses!"

"Must be good soil here," said Rocky, inching the car along.

"I think it's the humidity," said Rochelle, who was inclined to sweat. She fanned herself but kept her nose out the window so as to get a good look at the town.

"Is that the Chamber of Commerce? In the back of a tanning salon?"

"What the sign says."

"Wanna stop?" Rochelle was as eager as a kid hoping to get a Dairy Queen dip cone.

Rocky glanced at the car clock. He knew he'd have to pull an all-nighter to get his project done.

"Please? I'm not ready to go home yet. I love this little town. Maybe there's some stuff here that we haven't seen."

Rocky doubted it but indulged his city-bred

bride anyway. A bell hung on the inside doorknob jingled when he pushed open the door of the Chamber of Commerce and Tawny's Quick Tan Salon. The aroma of a burning vanilla candle and a just-eaten Lean Cuisine lunch wafted through the room. The place was quiet, and at the sound of the bell, Mayor Alfred Tinker's ample-bodied assistant, Faye Beth Newman, looked up from her crossword puzzle. Her face brightened and she rose to her feet.

"Come in! Welcome to Ella Louise. I'm sorry, but Mayor Tinker's at the festival right now. He's left me to hold down the fort. Have you two been out there? Good! Have a good time? I'm so glad. Did you taste the okra? How about the fritters? Aren't they to die for? Now, tell me where you two are from."

"Houston," Rochelle said. "We're from Houston."

"Wonderful! What can I do for you?"

"Do you have any information about interesting things to see around town?"

"Sure do. Come right over here to our Visitor Center." From a card table two steps away, Faye Beth plucked a four-color brochure, a map, and a "Welcome to Ella Louise" coffee mug for each of them. "Take your time; look around. Ella Louise is a wonderful town." She unfolded the brochure. "You'll want to see the library; it's in an old historic building. Then there's Big Rock

Monument, Lover's Leap Scenic Outlook, and the American Indian Arrowhead and Artifact Museum."

"Wow." Rocky's interest was caught. "An Indian museum? Here?"

"Sure is. And it is something to see. Chief Johnson built it in front of his house. Been five years, I guess."

"There's an Indian chief living in Ella Louise?"

"Oh, honey, not a real Indian," Faye Beth said with a wink. "His people's mostly Irish, I think. William Earl is his real name, but ever since he was a child, he's loved Indian stuff. Museum's open every Tuesday and Thursday afternoon. You'll know Chief when you see him. He's the only man in town what wears that Indian jewelry."

"Sure wish he was open today," Rocky said as he studied the brochure.

"Guess that just means y'all will have to come back," said Faye Beth. "We could use a pair of young folks like you. Why, you ought to just move yourselves up here."

Rocky and Rochelle went home; he to study, she to dream. Because after visiting Ella Louise, Rochelle, who had lived in the city all her life, decided she wanted to move there.

Every weekend, she tried to cajole Rocky into taking a drive back to Ella Louise. Most weekends his answer was the same. "Not today,

Rochelle. I've got to study." He was in his last and most time-consuming semester.

"Come on! You never want to do anything fun."

He winced at her words.

"Someday we're going to move there. I know it," Rochelle told him.

"Someday." But Rocky, keeper of their budget, didn't see how it could ever happen—especially if he didn't graduate and get a full-time job.

Then, six months after their visit to Ella Louise, Rochelle's great-aunt passed away. Soon as her will was read, Someday arrived. Rochelle was the woman's sole heir.

By then, Rocky had graduated. And he and Rochelle promptly moved to Ella Louise.

Faye Beth Newman took credit for Rocky and Rochelle's move. "I told those kids they should move here," she bragged. "They went and took me up on my invitation."

Rocky secured his first teaching job—social studies at Ella Louise Middle School. He spent hours at night preparing his lessons so as to be ready for the next day's classes.

Rocky's dedication to his work rankled Rochelle. She wanted to throw block parties, go shopping for curtain fabric, and take hikes along the creek. "Come on, Rocky! Let's do something spontaneous!"

He would, he'd tell her, just as soon as he finished his lesson plans and averaged all his students' end-of-semester grades.

After a few months in Ella Louise, Rochelle, who had learned how to cook in her great-aunt's kitchen, bought the town's old Dairy Queen, which had been closed for over a year. Rocky, after school and on weekends, helped her clean it, paint it, and fix it up. Once it was done, Rochelle hung a sign that said "Welcome to the Wild Flour Café" and began serving breakfast and lunch.

They also bought a tidy frame house—white with green trim—next door to the library. The house needed work, but Rocky fixed it up too. Months after moving in, he made a surprising discovery in the backyard. He'd finally had a free afternoon to spend cleaning up along their lot's back fence. Several seasons of fallen branches, tall grass, and climbing vines had nearly taken over the back half of the yard. "Rochelle, come look at this."

"What is it?"

"A well, I think."

"Like for water?"

"What it looks like."

"Does it have water in it?"

Turns out, it did.

The next day at the Wild Flour Café, Rochelle questioned Crow Buxley, one of her best breakfast customers.

"Crow, you know anything about the history of my place?"

Sure enough, he did. Place used to be in his family. Years and years ago.

Rochelle plied him with a slice of homemade pumpkin bread.

"Honey, there's a story about that well. When my great-grandparents settled on that place, wasn't no such thing as running water. My grandmother had to haul it in buckets, up from the creek."

"How long ago was that?" asked Rochelle.

"Hundred years, at least. Wasn't really much town here then. More like a settlement, I guess you'd say. Anyway, my great-grandfather George was crazy about my great-grandmother Lizzie. Growing up, the two of them lived neighbors. Played together when they was children."

"That's so romantic," gushed Rochelle.

"Well, one day when they was about seventeen and eighteen years old, George and Lizzie up and decided to get married. Them and a couple of their friends—they had to have witnesses—loaded up in George's daddy's wagon, drove over to the preacher's house, and sent someone in after him. The man came out and married them right there in the wagon."

"They didn't even get out?"

"Nope. Back in them days times were hard. People didn't make any big production out of everday events like they do now."

Rochelle hid a smile and poured Crow a glass of lemon iced tea.

"Anyways, they got hitched. For the first few years of their married life, they lived with George's folks. His mother wasn't well, and Lizzie was a big help to her. Then George's mother passed, and his daddy remarried. That was when George commenced to building them a little house on the same spot where yours sits now."

"And Lizzie had to haul water?"

"Yes. Hauling heavy water buckets wore even fleshy women out, and she was a tiny little thing. You can see her in old pictures. Ninety pounds soakin' wet'd be my guess. Now Lizzie didn't complain much; she just did what had to be done. But George decided he was gonna dig her a well."

"By hand?"

"All by hand. Weren't no drilling machines 'round here back then. He went at it with a pickax and a shovel. Dug through forty feet of rock. Took him four years 'cause he had to do all the digging when his other labor was done—and there was plenty of that. Didn't work on it ever day, just when he could."

Ten feet a year, figured Rochelle. "Four years? And he didn't give up? Did he ever wonder if he was digging in the right spot?"

"Sure he did. Took a lot of ribbin' from his neighbors. After the first year or two, they thought he was crazy to keep it up. And Lizzie—sweet a woman as she was—got tired of it too. Ever bit of his spare time, George was out digging. Many a time Lizzie would want to go visitin' her sister or she'd want to take a ride into town, but George wouldn't do it, because he had to work on that well. Just dig, dig, dig, ever minute he got."

"When he finally hit water, I bet George was really excited."

"He was. He'd been diggin' a couple hours when from the side of the well, down low, he noticed a real small trickle, so small that you 'bout couldn't see it. Four years, he'd been diggin'. That was the first sight of water he saw."

"I bet he called for Lizzie to come see."

"No. He kept it to hisself. The next day, when he climbed down in that well, the floor where he was digging was a little damp. By the end of the day—he let his other work go that day—it was muddy. He knew he was close, but still he didn't tell Lizzie. He had in mind a surprise. When he came in for dinner, she noticed that his boots was wet, and she questioned him about it. He told her he'd spilled water on them when he was washing up."

Rochelle poured Crow a second glass of tea.

"That night, George could hardly sleep, he was so excited. Next morning, he got up way before Lizzie did, when it was barely getting light outside, went out to the well, and climbed down inside it. And after just an hour of work, he found himself standing in six inches of water."

"Did he go get Lizzie then?"

"No, not then. What he did was creep into the house, careful not to let the screen door slam. He got a teacup out of the cupboard, run back out to the well, and filled the cup with water. Careful, so as not to spill it, for his hands were shaking something terrible, he carried it back into the house, knelt down beside the bed, woke Lizzie up, and showed her that cup of water."

Rochelle sighed. "What a sweet man. He must have loved her so much!"

"Yep," Crow went on. "George had dreamed of that moment for four years. The thought of bringing her that water was with him ever time he got down in that hole and picked up his shovel. The smile on her face was what he had waited for."

Rochelle sighed again, enthralled by Crow's romantic tale.

Crow pushed his plate back and drained his glass of tea. "Honey, I've got to get on home, but before I do, I'm gone let you in on a little secret that most women don't know. My great-grandpa George weren't all that special."

"What do you mean? He spent four long years digging a well for his wife!"

"Naw, now listen up. Sugar, most ever bit of

what a good man does is to please his woman. He may not dig her a well, or build her a mansion, or fight her a bear, but when he puts in overtime at work, feeling like he's come down with the flu, it's with her on his mind. When he's barely twenty years old and spends his Saturday mowing the yard, putting a new seat on the toilet, and changing the oil in the car, he's doing it for her. When he goes to the store because the baby got the diarrhea and needs diapers even though the score's tied and it's the bottom of the ninth, he's hoping she'll smile at him when he gets back. I'm telling you, a man won't let on, but pleasing his wife is the thing he wants most. That's all great-grandpa George was looking for when he spent four years diggin' that well that right now is sittin' in your backyard."

Rochelle couldn't think of what to say.

Crow scooted his chair back. "Now. How much do I owe you? Reckon you got change for a hundred?"

That evening after dinner, Rochelle asked Rocky to walk out with her so she could take another look at the well. Even in the twilight, she could see that he had repaired the rotten frame around it and had hung a shiny new bucket from a strong new rope.

"Looks nice," she said.

Rocky dropped the bucket down, let it fill, and then slowly pulled it up. "I took a sample in to be tested. Turns out this is good water. Pure enough to drink. Want a taste?"

"Sure."

Rocky dipped his cupped hands into the bucket and raised them to Rochelle's lips.

Water dribbled from his fingertips down her chin.

"Good?"

"Very. Best water I ever tasted."

He smiled.

She smiled.

They tell me that it is good water indeed.

2

Hot Dog's on the House

"What a pretty piece," gushed clinic nurse Janet Evans. "Esther, have you seen this?"

Esther Vaughn, the clinic's receptionist and farsighted, good-natured expert on most everything, pushed her reading glasses up on her nose so as to better study the tiny stitches. "I'm telling you. I've done a good bit of needlepoint myself, but never anything so intricate as this. Lots of work goes into a piece like that."

"Five months worth. That's how long Miss Annie said it took her to make it." Dr. Sarah Strickland, sole physician at Ella Louise's Family Medical Clinic, held the framed needlepoint at arm's length to see the full effect.

"Miss Annie gave it to you? Just now? What a sweet woman."

"Bless her sweet heart."

Indeed.

At the conclusion of her regular checkup, Miss Annie Wall, arthritic, diabetic, and experiencing what unfortunately looked like early symptoms of Alzheimer's, had thrust the unexpected gift upon Dr. Strickland. Sarah had responded appropriately, gently hugging Miss Annie and thanking her profusely. Yet though the tangible expression of Miss Annie's gratitude truly touched Sarah's heart, its message rankled.

"Goodness! Where you gonna hang it, Dr. Strickland?" asked Janet. "In the waiting room?"

"Not there," said Esther. "Way too much stuff cluttering up those walls already. I say we put it in the main exam room. There's that blank spot over the scales. Folks could use something nice to look at while they wait for you to give them the bad news!"

Janet giggled. "I say we hang it in the hall— next to the chart racks."

"I think there's a nail in my desk drawer. Want me to get the hammer, Doctor?"

"Wait just a second," Sarah hedged. "Let's don't hang it quite yet."

"Don't you like it?"

"Umm . . ."

"Don't you wanna hang it?"

"Umm . . ."

"Maybe she wants to take it home and display it in her house."

"Why, of course! What are we thinking? I'll wrap it up nice so the frame won't get scratched."

"Be cute in your den."

"Or in your bedroom."

"Perfect in your entry hall."

The truth?

The sampler would hang in none of those spots.

Sarah appreciated the lovingly crafted, gold-framed sampler. She did. She admired the workmanship. She liked the colors. She even thought the border design was especially nice. And she *loved* Miss Annie. What Sarah was less than crazy about was the sentimental, carefully stitched message.

It made her wince.

God Couldn't Be Everywhere That's Why He Made Mothers

Mothers.

Always there for their kids.

Always smiling.

Never too busy to bake cupcakes, read storybooks, or play cars.

Never tired, never irritable.

Never on call at the clinic.

Never, *ever* divorced.

Dr. Sarah Strickland, despite a calm professional manner, despite her competence and her compassion, grieved over what she perceived to be her numerous maternal failings. Becoming a single parent had never been in her plans.

Bless Miss Annie's sweet heart, indeed. Sarah did not need a needlepoint reminder of what she could never be.

Sarah tucked the framed gift into her tote bag. *It'll make a nice Mother's Day gift for my mother,* she mused with a bit of sarcasm. Mom never worked outside the home. Mom never got divorced. Mom's parenting skills put June Cleaver to shame.

After her 3:00 appointment Sarah called to check on her twelve-year-old twins. This was the first summer that she'd allowed the boys to stay at home without a sitter. Though they groaned at her repeated safety instructions and reminders not to open the door to anyone while she was gone, and though they told her over and over again that they were *not babies,* Sarah was worried about them.

And called them. At least every hour or so.

"Everything okay, Josh? Good. You had lunch? Kevin too? Potpies? You ate them frozen? Honey, you're supposed to cook them in the microwave! I'm not sure they're safe to eat like that. Was the chicken cooked? Are you sure? Okay. Clean up your mess. Put your dishes in the washer. Let me speak to Kevin.

"Kevin? You all right? Good. Nope. No swimming until I get home. About six. Did you get your chores done? All of them?

"What about Georgia? Did you feed her? There's a fresh bag of dog food in the garage. Feed her first, then bathe her. Yes. Today. Before I get home. Georgia had better be clean when I get home or there won't be any swimming. I mean it. See you in a few hours. Love you. Bye."

Janet and Esther, whose kids were all grown up, eavesdropped, stifled giggles, and felt sympathy for their boss. Both of them remembered the trials they'd been through when their kids were at home and they were at work.

"I used to worry all day that they'd set the house on fire or something."

"My two used to fight. I'd just pray every hour that they wouldn't draw blood."

"Your boys will be fine," they assured Sarah after the frozen potpie incident. "It's good for them to have a little time by themselves. Helps them to grow up and be independent. Don't you worry. Take care of your patients. If one of your boys calls and it can't wait, we'll come and get you."

But it wasn't a call from one of the boys that precipitated Janet and Esther scuttering like flustered hens into the exam room, where Dr. Strickland was tending her last patient of the day—a skinny little man who had a big wart on the second finger of his left hand.

"Excuse me," Janet said to the patient. "Dr. Strickland, you better come here."

"What's the matter? Copy machine acting up again? Can't it wait?"

"No. Copy machine's fine. There's an officer here. He says he's just come from your house, and he needs to see you right now," Esther said.

"Mr. Stevens," Janet told the befuddled and already disinfected patient, "can you wait just a minute? Here's a magazine for you to read. Dr. Strickland will be right back."

When Sarah saw the uniformed officer standing in the waiting room, nervously shifting from one foot to the other, holding his hat in his hand, she knew deep within her heart that her worst fears were about to be confirmed.

The news had to be bad.

I should never have left the boys alone, she thought. *I should have made them go to day care no matter how much they protested. What was I thinking? Fact is, I should have let the practice go for the summer and stayed home with them. But then how would I have kept us afloat financially? This is what I get. I should never have agreed to the divorce. That's it! No. I should have never married their father in the first place. Why, I should have become a teacher instead of a doctor! Teachers have summers off. What kind of a mother leaves her babies alone at home in a world full of violence and crime?*

Keeping her panicked thoughts to herself and feigning a physician's well-practiced calm, Sarah looked the officer in the eye and asked right out, "Tell me. What is it? Are my boys hurt?"

"Ma'am," said the officer, "I don't know anything about your boys."

"You don't! Then who does?"

"Ma'am, I'm here about your dog."

Her dog? Her boys? What was going on?

"I'm the new animal control officer. Todd Scutter. Moved here with my wife, Patricia. I don't deal with boys. Just dogs. Cats too. Well, and rabbits sometimes. Even a snake or two on occasion . . ."

What? The boys were okay? Professional calm forgotten, Sarah sank into a chair. Esther got out a manila folder and fanned her while Janet went for a glass of water.

"Uh, ma'am, do you live at twelve-thirteen Garden Patch Road?"

"Yes, but—"

"Then I've got the right person. Seems we've got us a little problem. It's not that there's no ordinance against keeping your dog on the roof of your house, but ma'am, your poor pooch is barking her head off up there. Pitch of that roof's pretty steep. Isn't much in the way of shade. I don't think she's too happy, and neither are your neighbors. Three of 'em called city hall to fuss about it. I tried the doorbell at your house but didn't get any answer."

No answer at the door. Of course. Both boys knew better than to answer the door when she wasn't home.

Wait a minute. There was a dog on the roof of her house? Georgia? What was Georgia doing up there?

"Someone told me you would be working here, so that's why I'm calling on you at your place of business. Ma'am, do you think you could find some other place to keep your dog?"

You bet she could.

After finishing up with Mr. Stevens's wart ("Put antibiotic ointment on it twice a day and keep it covered with a bandage. Sorry you had to wait."), Sarah drove home. Sure enough, perched on the roof of the house, alternately whining, panting, pawing, and barking, was poor Georgia. Unable to lie down without losing her balance and tumbling to the ground, she nervously paced back and forth. Though she looked completely worn out, when she saw Sarah, her stumpy tail began to wag.

"Hold on, girl. Just give me a minute, and I'll get you down." Sarah got a ladder from the garage, leaned it up against the side of the house, climbed to the top, and brought the shaky-legged dog down to safety. Sarah released Georgia into the fenced backyard of the house, then waved at the nosy neighbors across the street.

Engrossed in a video game, Kevin and Josh didn't even look up when Sarah walked into the house.

"Hi, Mom."

"Hi, Mom."

"What's for dinner?"

"Can we go swimming now?"

She turned off the game.

"Mom! Why'd you do that? I was way ahead."

"Why you got a mad look on your face, Mom? We did our chores."

"We cleaned up the kitchen."

"Picked up our clothes."

"We even gave Georgia her bath."

"And where is Georgia?" asked Sarah.

"Uh-oh." The twins looked at each other.

"Just a second, Mom; I need to get something from outside." Kevin got up to go outside.

"Too late. I already got her down. Can you tell me how exactly Georgia got up on the roof?"

"We put her there."

"Guys, why would you do that?"

"You told us to bathe her."

"You said she had to be clean when you got home."

"So we put her up there to keep her from getting dirty."

"Did you smell her, Mom? She smells pretty good."

"For a dog."

After a moment's pause, Sarah's tense shoulders relaxed. The furrow in her brow smoothed. The churning in her stomach slowed. She bent and gave her boys big hugs before allowing that Georgia did indeed smell pretty good.

For a dog.

• • •

There would be time to correct their misdeed. Time for Sarah to teach her boys yet more stuff about safety and pet care and how they must never, ever climb on a ladder when she wasn't home.

But all that would have to wait for another day. On this one, Sarah, like Georgia, was simply going to enjoy the exquisite feeling of having her feet set back on the ground.

3

Let Her Eat Cake

"Chamber of Commerce. Yes. Yes. Can you hold on a minute, please?" Faye Beth Newman held her freshly manicured hand over the mouthpiece of the phone. "Mayor," she hissed, "it's Windell Minter. He wants to know if you're still here."

"What does he need?" Mayor Tinker already had his coat on. The phone had rung just as he was about to leave the office an hour early, which, forever mindful of giving a day's work for a day's taxpayer pay, he never, ever did.

"Says he needs to talk to you about getting a permit to build a slide of some kind."

Shoot. Today was Mayor Tinker's wife, Tiny's, birthday. He'd hoped to get home from work before she did so that he could have dinner ready when she drove in. He'd had it all planned since last week. Pork loin, red potatoes, asparagus, sugar-free buttermilk pie. All of her favorites. Taking Windell Minter's call would mean a delay of no telling how long. Feeling guilty, he shifted from one foot to the other and looked at his watch.

Ten till five.

Then without giving Alfred the chance to decide, Faye Beth spoke into the phone. "Windell, I'm sorry, but you've just missed the mayor. He had some business to take care of and left early. How about I put you down for first thing in the morning? That will be fine. Okay. I'll sure tell him." She hung up the phone.

"Faye Beth—" the mayor began.

"Shush. Get yourself out that door. Go on now, before Windell drives by and sees you're still here. You've put in at least forty-five hours this week already—what with city council and library board meetings. It won't hurt a thing for you to scoot out early. Why, if they paid it, the city would owe you overtime. Go home. Make Tiny a good dinner. Tell her that I said to have a happy birthday. You baking her a sugar-free cake?"

All the way home, Mayor Tinker stewed. A slide? Whatever did Windell Minter want a slide for? He was a bachelor with no kids. Even if he did have kids, they'd be too old for a slide. Best Mayor Tinker could recall, Windell didn't have any young nieces or nephews either. And what was the deal with Windell thinking he needed a permit? Why, nearly every third house in Ella Louise had a minivan parked in the driveway. From where he sat, looked like the one command from God that young couples of Ella Louise had taken to heart was to be fruitful and multiply. Minivans were what mamas and daddies these days used to cart their kids from one place to another. And anyone with sense would know that where there's a minivan, there's gonna be a Sears Best swing set—with a seesaw and a slide—set up in the backyard.

A permit? For a slide?

Faye Beth must have heard Windell wrong.

But she had not.

"No, Mayor," said Windell the next morning, "not a kid's playground slide. I'm talking about one of those big yellow slides—high as a four-story building—where customers climb up, sit down on a tow sack, and slide down fast as greased pigs."

"Like at the fair?"

"That's right." Windell was so excited that he sat on the edge of his seat, rapping his diamond pinkie ring on the mayor's desk as he spoke. "My cousin Eddie put one in down in Houston. Folks pay two dollars apiece for the chance to slide. It doesn't take 'em more'n about thirty seconds, tops. You do the math. This thing is going to be a money magnet. I realize that two dollars may sound steep, but I aim to offer group rates. Senior citizen discounts too."

Wonderful, thought the mayor. *Ella Louise's elderly are going to be lining up in droves to climb four flights of stairs so as to hurl their arthritic bodies to the ground.* He struggled not to chuckle at the thought of the Senior Citizen Care Van making a stop at Windell's slide.

"So. Do I need a permit?" asked Windell.

"Yes. For something like that you do. Where exactly are you planning on putting this slide thing?" He coughed. "Windell—you're not planning on building it yourself, are you?" He was thinking of how Windell's do-it-himself carport had turned out.

"No. Course not. I've got an outfit from Oklahoma coming. Man says that they'll haul it in pieces on three big trucks. Take a week to ten days to assemble the thing. As for where I'm putting it, well, get this." Windell stood for effect. "The town of Ella Louise can look for Windell's Super Slide to go in right next to Lindell's Clean-It-Quick Car Wash." He sat back down. "Way he and I figure it, folks these days are busy, always looking to kill two birds with one stone. This way, they can have some fun at my place, then go right next door to my brother's and take care of cleaning their car. Lindell's all excited about it. He's planning on getting some new sprayers for two of his bays, and's even talking about putting a cappuccino machine in for folks who have to wait."

"That's quite a plan."

"We're real excited about it, Mayor, but I haven't told you the best part."

41

"No?"

"Our sister, Daphne, is moving back to Ella Louise so as to help us out at both places."

"Daphne? Is she, I mean, how is she . . . ?"

Windell stopped tapping his ring. He ran his fingers over his almost-bald head, then folded them in his lap and leaned back in his chair. "Mayor, Daphne's made it sixty-six days without a drink. The doc at the place where me and Lindell put her this time says that she's done real good. Soon as she's got a job lined up—that's one of the requirements, that they have a set job before they get out—me and Lindell can bring her back home."

"Bless her heart. She going to stay by herself or with you and Lindell?"

"With us. Less temptation. We're gonna sell her place over in Pearly."

"Windell, sounds like you've got a good plan, but I'm wondering, do you think it's safe for Daphne to . . . ?"

"Don't worry, Mayor. We're gonna keep a good eye on her. Me and Lindell'll have her making change, refilling the soap dispensers in the restrooms, handing out two-for-one coupons. Stuff like that."

"I see," said the mayor. "I certainly wish her the best. You know, Daphne went to school with my baby brother. She was a cute little kid. It's been hard to see the turn she's taken. You and Lindell have been real good to her."

"Family's family, and she's the only sister we've got," Windell said as he shrugged.

"Is she going to church?"

"No. She won't set foot in the door."

"Too bad. It'd help if she would."

"I know it. But ever time I try to talk to her about it, she says she's not interested. Claims there's too many hypocrites in churches."

Mayor Tinker laughed. "She's got that right. Ever church I know of is full of sinners. Too bad she doesn't understand that's the whole point. I'll be praying for her."

"Appreciate it. Daphne is a good person. At least she never took drugs. We're thankful for that. Maybe this time around she'll give it a go." Windell stood. "So—you think I'll have any trouble getting that permit?"

"No. None at all. I'll call down to City Hall and let them know to expect you."

"Thanks, Mayor." Windell had his hand on the door. "I almost forgot. Lindell and I are planning a big ribbon-cutting and grand opening. I'd be honored if you'd be the one to come down and do the cutting. I'll even see to it that you get to take the first trip down my slide—at no cost, of course."

Mayor Tinker hated heights. Moving past the third step of a ladder made his feet hurt so bad that Faye Beth had to be the one to change the lightbulbs in the Chamber of Commerce restrooms. "Thank you, Windell. Kind of you to ask. I'll take a look at my book. Faye Beth keeps me pretty busy, but I'll do my best to be there. Have a good day, now."

When Pastor Joseph Tedford of Chosen Vessel (Ella Louise's only nondenominational church) heard of Daphne Minter's impending arrival in town, when he learned of her *problem*—as it was delicately referred to at the monthly meeting of the Ministerial Alliance—he felt a stirring in his heart. When he heard of her reported disinterest in church attendance, he felt not discouraged but challenged. And a little bit afraid.

So he began to pray.

Which was a good thing.

Daphne Minter (who, after a fifth divorce, decided to keep her maiden name to save herself a lot of future trouble), was released from the rehab hospital on her thirty-sixth birthday, one week before Halloween, which just happened to be her very favorite holiday.

To celebrate their sister's homecoming as well as her birthday, Lindell baked Daphne a coconut cake and Windell brought home some flowers— pink carnations with baby's breath in a clear bud vase tied up with a variegated ribbon. They also went in together and got her some stationery and a bottle of cucumber-scented hand lotion, a fragrance choice that Windell questioned until the salesgirl told him that cucumber was among their most popular scents. "That and water-melon," she said.

Daphne liked her gifts. Despite the weirdness of the first night in her brothers' house, and despite dealing with them watching her every move, enduring their unspoken desires, guarded expectations, and prayers that *this* time, please, she would be okay, her first night went well.

Until the subject of Halloween came up.

"What do you mean, you don't celebrate Halloween?" Daphne asked. "No candy? No parties? You don't even dress up?"

No. They didn't. But there was a nice community-wide Harvest Festival at their church. Food, fun, and fellowship. Wouldn't she like to go?

Would there be costumes?

Uh, no.

Scary decorations?

No again.

Pumpkins?

Why, yes! Always.

Carved?

Uh, sorry. No.

She thought she would pass.

Of course, just because her brothers held to crazy notions about Halloween being some-thing bad didn't mean that she had to go along. Hadn't they said that this was her house too? That she was to make herself at home? Then she would. She'd be a witch, would carve a pumpkin, and would hand out candy. Lots of candy.

So there.

Windell and Lindell were mindful of their sister's precarious state. They'd been warned by her doctor that the upcoming holidays would be when she would most likely slip. Stress, they were told. Expectations. Memories of times past. And while Windell and Lindell had already thought ahead to how they would help Daphne make it through Thanksgiving, Christmas, and New Year's, they had never considered that Halloween would be a problem.

They agreed it was best not to get Daphne stirred up.

"What's it going to hurt?" said Windell to Lindell after Daphne had gone up to bed.

"I agree," said Lindell. "It's not worth the risk. Let her have her way this year. Next year, we can take a stronger stand."

As Halloween approached, Daphne got as excited as a kid about her costume, the treats she would hand out, and how she planned to decorate the porch and the yard.

All well and good, up to a point. Windell and Lindell, despite their agreement to look the other way for the sake of their sister's sobriety, felt forced to put their feet down when Daphne proposed putting in a fake cemetery, complete with cardboard coffins, next to the fall garden.

"Okay," Daphne threw up her hands. "No cemetery. How about some artificial cobwebs hanging from the trees?"

Windell and Lindell both sighed.

On Halloween night, after Lindell and Windell left to go to the church festival, Daphne put on her costume. She'd worked on it for the past two days and thought it looked pretty good. She had a long black dress—made from Lindell's old college graduation gown—a black pointed hat, black stockings and shoes, and even fake black teeth. Only her face didn't look the part. *Not scary enough,* thought Daphne. What to do?

She didn't wear makeup. There was none in the house. Maybe some flour from the kitchen would give her the pale glow she was looking for. She tried patting some on, but within minutes, it had all worn off. Shoe polish maybe? All she found on the shelf was a color called "Burnished Brown."

Maybe not.

When Daphne stepped outside to check on her pumpkins, the flickering green-white glow of late-season fireflies flitting just above the grass caught her eyes. That was just the color she wanted for her face. What would happen if a person rubbed firefly juice on something? Would it glow? Made sense that it would. And wouldn't it look cool!

Daphne hunted in the kitchen cabinet above the sink until she found an empty mayonnaise jar. That would work.

Chasing fireflies made Daphne sweat. She'd aimed for ten, but gave up, out of breath, when she had six. Fireflies were harder to catch than one might think. The little critters were only visible when lit, and they flew up, down, and from side to side quickly, making no sound.

Once back inside the house, Daphne held the jar up and studied the bugs. This was the hard part. They looked awfully pretty, their little lights flickering off and on. Seemed kind of sad. Maybe she should forget about this, take them outside, and let them go. There was time to run down to the drugstore for makeup. *But no,* she thought, *a bug is a bug. No difference between a firefly and a housefly.*

Where did her brothers keep the flyswatter, anyway?

When the first trick-or-treaters came to the Minter door, they were greeted by a very scary, glowing, if somewhat streaky, Witch Daphne.

"Wow! How did you get your face to look like that?" asked a costumed beggar.

"Is that makeup?" asked another.

"What makes it light up?"

"Ha, ha, ha! I'll never tell!" cackled Daphne. The effect was even better than she'd hoped for. She plucked bags of treats from a smoking black caldron she had rigged with dry ice. "What do you say?"

"Trick or treat!" they chorused.

"What else?"

"Thank you."

"You're welcome. Be careful. Don't knock over my pumpkins."

Across town at the Harvest Festival, Joseph Tedford's son won a chocolate pecan layer cake at the cakewalk. "Say 'thank you,' Isaac," Joseph prompted. Isaac complied even though, because he was allergic to chocolate, he wouldn't be able to eat a bite.

"Mr. Minter," Joseph said (for the life of him, he never could remember which brother was which). "Good to see you. How's your sister doing? She here tonight?"

"Fine," answered Lindell once he'd restarted the tape that set the cake-craving walkers in motion. "She's doing fine so far. Thank you for asking. I wish I could say that she was here, but she stayed home to do Halloween."

"That's too bad. I was hoping to meet her. I'd like to come and visit, invite her to my church— that is, if you don't mind," Joseph said. Then he added quickly, "She's not already a church member, is she?" (Stealing a member from another church in town was greatly frowned upon by members of the Ministerial Alliance. It had even been discussed at last month's meeting. "Gentlemen," Brother Fred from First Baptist had exhorted, "there are enough sinning sheep in this town to go around. No need in any of us carrying off members of each other's flocks.")

"No, Daphne's not been a churchgoer since we were kids. You feel free to come on over anytime—but be warned. Talk about church sometimes gets my sister riled up. And when Daphne gets riled up, she isn't always nice!"

On the way home, sleepy son in tow, Joseph thought of taking the chocolate cake to Daphne. Why not? It was a perfect excuse. Everyone likes cake, even folks who think that they don't like church. He'd give it to her, invite her to services, and be on his way. Perfect.

Within an hour of smearing the remains of the dead fireflies' bottoms on her face, Daphne Minter was in a mess. She had not known that this would happen. Her whole face was swollen, and even though she'd scrubbed and scrubbed to get the dried goo off, her skin burned like fire. Too miserable to hand out candy, she lay down on the couch with a wet cloth over her eyes.

She'd only just hit the cushions when someone rang the doorbell. She ignored it, but they rang again and again. She'd turned off the porch light. Couldn't they take a hint? She groaned as she dragged herself up from the couch.

"Excuse me," said Joseph when Daphne finally cracked the door open. "Daphne Minter?"

"Yes?"

"I'm Pastor Joseph. From Chosen Vessel Church. Little white building on Magnolia Street?"

"What do you want?"

"I brought you a cake. My son won it at the cakewalk but he can't eat it, and I thought you might like it."

"A cake?" She'd had no dinner. "Just a minute. Let me turn on the light."

"Long as I'm here, I'd also like to invite you to . . . oh my goodness! What's wrong with your face?"

"Nothing. It's nothing." Daphne looked down and tried to shield her eyes with her hand.

"Do you need some help? Should I go get one of your brothers?"

No, she did not want her brothers. She didn't want the religious tract that Joseph tried to hand her, either. And she especially didn't want Joseph's special invitation to attend his church. As for the cake? It looked good. She would take the cake. "Good-bye." Daphne closed the door on Joseph's face.

●　●　●

When Dr. Sarah Strickland prescribed soothing salve and prescription pain pills for Daphne Minter, she thought she was doing the right thing. "You mean you actually crushed fireflies and rubbed them on your face? Whatever for?"

"To look scary. For Halloween. I was a witch."

"Did it work?" asked Dr. Strickland.

"It did. My face glowed like a firefly. But only for a little while. Then it wore off."

In all her years of practice, Sarah had not seen anything quite like the awful blisters on Daphne's face. She was obviously in terrible pain.

"Take one every six hours. I want to see you back in my office three days from now."

The pain pills helped, but they weren't quite strong enough. Daphne hurt something awful. Neither Lindell nor Windell was keeping count of the pills, so she was able to swallow two at a time, and every four hours instead of six. Unfortunately, this made the pills run out too fast, and she was forced to drive Lindell's mustard-colored El Camino to the next town in order to purchase a bottle of wine. She needed something to tide her over until she could get more pills from Dr. Strickland. She only bought one bottle of wine, and it was only to ease the pain, not much different from an aspirin, she told herself. Everything would be okay once Dr. Strickland gave her a refill.

Except she didn't.

"Looking good," said Dr. Strickland. "I don't believe you'll have any scarring, which surprises me. You're healing quite nicely. More pills? No. I don't think so. You can take some Tylenol if you feel like you need it, but I don't think you will."

Daphne drove directly from Dr. Strickland's office to the closest across-the-county-line liquor store and stocked up.

Windell and Lindell were beside themselves when they got home and found out what she'd done. Not even dry a week. Should they take her back to the hospital? Try to reason with her?

So numb with disappointment were the brothers that they pretty much gave up. At least their sister was staying with them for now. She wouldn't end up on the street. If they couldn't keep her dry, at least they could keep her safe.

When word of Daphne's backslide got around town, she was put on the prayer list of every Ella Louise congregation. No one was terribly shocked, though. It was God the poor thing needed. Power from above. No way was she going to lick this thing until she saw her need of him.

One by one, all the ministers in town came to talk to Daphne about her soul. Brother Fred came by. She told him where he could go. Pastor

Graves stopped in. She suggested that he put his Bible in a very dark place.

When Joseph Tedford came, he brought cake.

Which Daphne ate. Twice a week.

"Daphne," Joseph said at the end of each visit, "God loves you. This Sunday, why don't you come pay a visit to his house?"

"Uh-uh. Reverend Joe, that's not gonna happen," she said, wiping crumbs from her chin. "Not this week or the next. You're just wasting your time."

"No, I'm not," he answered each time. "God doesn't give up, and neither will I."

On a Tuesday morning, after three months of his discouraging biweekly visits to Daphne, Joseph was sitting in his office at the back of the church (not studying his Bible as was later reported in the paper, but working a crossword puzzle, if the truth be known) when he heard an awful crash. It shook the roof and walls. An earthquake? Never happened before in Ella Louise. A bomb then! Joseph jumped from his chair, unsure whether to run out of the building or to take cover inside.

Then he heard a roaring sound. Was it a tornado? How? The skies were clear. Then Joseph smelled smoke. When he saw that it was coming from the hallway to the sanctuary, he ran to see.

There was so much smoke surrounding the scene that for a moment Joseph couldn't take it all in. Pews were pushed forward. The communion table was on its side. Broken glass and splintered wood were everywhere. Daylight streamed in from a gaping hole made in the back wall.

In the middle of his sanctuary sat a car—a yellow El Camino. Its engine was still running.

Joseph had to climb over pews and debris to get to the passenger door. When he did, he reached in the open window, over and across the driver, and turned off the car.

He placed his hand on the slumped-over-the-wheel driver. "Daphne. Are you hurt?"

"No." There wasn't a mark on her. "Where am I?"

Joseph could not suppress a grin. "Daphne, my friend, you are in the exact place the Lord and I have been trying to get you for three months. Too bad you didn't see fit to use the door. Welcome to Chosen Vessel. Like what we've done to the place? Come on. Let me help you out. Let's go into my office and have some cake."

I'd like to report that Daphne Minter has trod the straight and narrow ever since the day she drove into Joseph's church.

She hasn't.

Daphne's path to sobriety has been one marked by twists and turns, complicated detours, and maddening switchbacks. Just about the time it seems she has her problem licked, she slips up.

Likely she will for the rest of her life.

But since the day of the accident—divine appointment is what Joseph calls it—Daphne has been going to Chosen Vessel Church. Every Sunday. She's learning to pray, and she's started reading from Psalms. She believes that God is helping her, and so she's decided to help him out too.

Five days a week and half a day on Saturday, Daphne works for Lindell and Windell down at the car wash and slide. She stays pretty busy, running the cash register, emptying the trash, filling the soap dispensers—and, piece by piece, handing out cake.

4

Magic Money

"Faye Beth, you had extra cheese on your hamburger."

"But I had water to drink."

"Janet, didn't you have dessert?"

"Uh-huh. The peach cobbler."

"With ice cream," said Faye Beth. "Don't forget to figure in the ice cream."

"Esther and I shared it," reminded Janet.

"Janet, you had coffee *and* iced tea. We just had tea."

Rochelle Shartle, who stood in her spot behind the cash register of the Wild Flour Café, was privy to the just-lunched ladies' efforts at math. She'd heard such tabletop reckoning at least a couple hundred times before. Rochelle hated to say it (and wouldn't to a man), but women are the worst when it comes to figuring out how to split a check. They'll nitpick over who had what for fifteen minutes or more when, after all is said and done, their individual meals will come within fifty cents of each other.

"Everything all right? Did you enjoy your

lunch? How were the rolls today?" Rochelle smiled as the women placed dollars, dimes, and pennies in the palm of her hand. No surprise—they'd come with exact change. "You gals come back. I'll be frying up catfish on Friday. Don't forget."

After the women made their trips to the rest-room, collected their jackets, and went out to their cars, Rochelle's new employee, nineteen-year-old Melissa Bates—who only this month moved to Ella Louise—moved quickly to clear their table, ready it for the next diner, and collect her tips.

"They're usually pretty generous," said Rochelle. "How about today?"

"Pretty good. About a dollar apiece," Melissa answered. "Except for the one with black hair. She left fifty cents."

"Esther," Rochelle said with feigned indignation. "And she had the pie! Speaking of which, let's you and I sit down and have a piece. I'm pooped, and we won't likely get another chance today."

It was almost 3:00. The café was empty, but the early-supper crowd would begin to trickle in just after 4:00.

"Melissa, pour me a glass of milk, will you? You want a Coke? I'll get the pie. What kind you want?"

The two of them sat down at a table away from the door. Rochelle quickly forked down a good portion of her pie and gulped half a glass of milk. She leaned back in her chair, closed her eyes, and took several long breaths. "Feels good to relax for a minute, doesn't it?" She opened her eyes and studied Melissa's feet. "Those shoes you're wearing don't look very comfortable. Do your feet hurt?"

Rochelle wasn't sure Melissa had heard her. The weary girl (she was working two jobs) sat with her knees together and shoulders hunched, only picking at her pie.

"Honey, is something bothering you?" Rochelle noticed that her only employee looked sort of red in the face. "You feeling okay?"

Melissa looked up and put her hand to her back. "I think I've got a bladder infection."

"Oh, those things are wretched! Why didn't you say something? I'll call Rocky to come up and help out with the supper crowd. Have you called Dr. Strickland for an appointment?"

"No. I'll be okay. I've been drinking lots of water and some cranberry juice too."

"Girl, if you've got a bladder infection, it is not going to get better by itself. Let me feel your forehead. Lean over."

Melissa did as she was told.

"You've got a fever. I'm calling the clinic and telling them that they'll need to work you in right now. Won't take you five minutes to get from here to there."

"I appreciate it," said Melissa, "but please don't. I'm broke. Even if I could afford to pay for an office visit, I wouldn't be able to get a prescription filled. I've had these things before. Lots of water, some aspirin—I'll get over it."

Rochelle studied Melissa for just a moment, then without a word got up and went to the cash register. From an envelope stuck behind the register, she retrieved a worn hundred dollar bill. Sitting back down, she slid the bill across the table, then took a big bite of her pie.

"Thank you, but I can't."

"Sure you can." Rochelle's legs were crossed. She swung her foot.

"There's no way that I can pay you back."

"It's not a loan." Rochelle took a swig of milk.

"I can't take a gift. You're my boss. It wouldn't be right."

"It's not a gift." After one last bite of pie, Rochelle wiped her mouth and laid her napkin down.

Melissa, who was weary and worried and trying her best not to fall apart in front of her employer, did not know what to do. She tore the paper wrapper from her straw into tiny bits and stacked them neatly beside her plate.

"See this envelope?" said Rochelle. The envelope was dingy and one corner was torn. On the outside were the words "Magic Money."

Melissa had no idea what the words meant.

She only knew she needed to go to the bathroom.

"Remember when I told you about me and Rocky moving here back when I was just nineteen?"

"That was when your great-aunt died and you used the money she left you to get your house and this restaurant."

"That's right, God bless her soul. Rocky had just finished up with college, and we were barely making ends meet. Then I got the money from my great-aunt. Even though it's worked out, looking back, we were crazy to spend all her money at one time like that, but we thought we had it figured to the penny. Before we decided for sure, we sat down together on the floor of our little apartment, and we wrote it all down. After paying for both places, the little house and the business, we would have five hundred dollars left to live on until he got his first check from the school. It would be tough, but we thought that we could make it work."

"Sounds like you had it all thought out."

"We did, except for one thing. On the day that we were to finish with all the paperwork, Rocky and I showed up with a cashier's check from the bank for exactly what we'd agreed to pay for the house and the business. We forgot one thing. Closing costs. Neither one of us had even heard of that. Four hundred and thirty-five more dollars was what we owed."

"What did you do?"

"We should have backed out right then, but we were both too embarrassed. Before he caught himself, Rocky blurted out something like, 'That leaves us sixty-five dollars to live on for a month!' "

"He said that?" Melissa giggled.

"Right there in front of all those lawyers and other important folks. I wanted to crawl under the table. Everybody just sort of coughed and looked around, but me and Rocky—well, I don't know what we were thinking, but we went ahead and signed all the papers. Once we were done, we took the keys to our new house and went right on over so we could get it clean enough to move in to. No one had lived in it for several years, so there was a lot of dust and stuff. We got busy sweeping and wiping, but I think we were both in shock. How were we going to get the utilities turned on? How were we going to eat? Put gas in our car? When you move, there are a lot of expenses. We'd already given word that we'd be out of our apartment in three days."

"You guys were in a real mess! You had no family to help?"

"Both of us come from families poorer than us. No way could we even let them know that we needed help."

"I know exactly what that's like. Can you hold on a second while I go to the bathroom?" Melissa sprinted to the ladies room and came back with sweat on her brow.

"Okay. I can tell, I've got to get to the point. That first night, Rocky and I were unloading our stuff and three cars pulled up into our driveway. We had met a few folks around town. One of them was Faye Beth Newman."

"Doesn't she work for the mayor?"

"That's her. She was one of the ladies that had lunch today. Part of the threesome that just left."

"Frosted hair? Pink blouse with the rhinestone trim?"

"That's her. The three that were here were the same three that showed up at our house. Faye Beth Newman, Janet Evans, and Esther Vaughn. In our driveway. And we didn't know what for."

"They look like sweet women. I bet they brought you a casserole or something."

"Yes, and a cake too. But that wasn't the only reason they'd come. It was Faye Beth, I think, who handed Rocky the envelope. She told him to take it, to open it, and to see what was inside. He nearly died when he saw that it was five hundred dollars."

"No!"

"Yes. It was. Word had gotten to them about the straits we were in. Rocky didn't know what to say. First he tried to give the money back. They wouldn't take it. Then he told them thank you.

They said that we were welcome. Then I promised them that we would pay it back. They said no."

"Five hundred dollars is a lot of money."

"It is. But you know what? Even though we could have paid them back—it would have just taken us a while, but we could've done it—they wouldn't hear of it. All three of them said that it was 'Magic Money,' not meant to be paid back but to be passed on. The only thing they told us was that they expected us to pass on that exact amount to other folks who were in need."

Rochelle and Melissa looked up to see two cars pull up close to the café door. Customers. It was time to get back to work.

But Rochelle placed her hand on Melissa's arm before Melissa had a chance to get up. "That was six years ago. Melissa, this hundred is the last of that five. I've kept it in an envelope and given it out whenever I saw a need. Some folks have needed just ten dollars, others twenty. Today, you need a hundred. This should be enough for your office visit and prescription. If it's not, I'll give you some more."

Melissa began to weep. "Thank you. Thank you so much."

"You're welcome. Don't you want this envelope?"

Turns out, Melissa did have a raging bladder infection. Dr. Strickland said it was a good thing that she came in. Once she got about a day's worth of antibiotics in her system, she got over the infection just fine.

What she didn't get over was Rochelle's generosity and the tale of the Magic Money. Today, Melissa still has the envelope. It's even more ragged looking than it was when Rochelle gave it to her. Even though she's taped it up on all sides, Melissa has taken to putting it inside a Ziploc plastic bag for extra protection.

The envelope is ragged because Melissa opens and closes it every payday and some days in between. She puts money into it when she gets paid, and she takes money out of it when she sees someone in need.

There's something funny about the whole thing. It's been five years, and that envelope has never run out of money. Not even close. That seems like a pretty amazing thing to me. But Melissa? When I ask, she tells me that she doesn't think too much about it. She just considers herself blessed to walk around every day knowing that there is magic in her purse.

5

Spanish Lessons

Because she was loath to raise his repeatedly dashed hopes, thirty-three-year-old Patricia Scutter didn't tell her husband, Todd, that she thought she might be pregnant.

After more than a decade of childless years, Patricia knew better. For the first few years of their marriage, she and Todd had tried to make a baby on their own.

But nothing happened.

Back then, they weren't too worried. Being high-achieving, ready-to-take-on-any-challenge firstborns, they read a few books and articles and concentrated their efforts.

Still nothing.

It was not until months of trying turned into five years of trying—with zero results—that Todd and Patricia sought the help of the specialists at a fertility clinic.

What an ordeal that turned out to be! Neither Todd nor Patricia was prepared for the humiliating, painful, and bank-breaking fertility tests and treatments that the doctors prescribed. Todd and Patricia endured getting stuck, poked, prodded, scanned, and sampled. But then quickly—way more quickly than they'd been led to expect—all discomfort and embarrassment were forgotten. Neither Todd nor Patricia had any doubts that all they'd been through had been worthwhile when, within three months of beginning treatments, Patricia became pregnant.

According to the doctors, her off-kilter reproductive system had just needed a bit of tweaking. ("Like Uncle Freddy's old Ford," Todd teased, hiding his relief that the blame for their infertility had not fallen on him.) Celebrating the good news with toasts of apple cider in wine glasses, Patricia and Todd wondered why they had waited so long to seek help. What *had* they been thinking? Medical science had truly come through.

And life was good until, early in her third month, Patricia suffered a miscarriage.

"Try not to worry," Todd and Patricia were told by professionally sympathetic physicians. "Happens in a high percentage of first pregnancies. Miscarriage occurs so often that it's hardly considered abnormal. Having one is not necessarily an indication that there's anything wrong. Try again. Next time will most likely result in a healthy child."

And so Patricia and Todd did try again.

And again.

And again.

Actually, they produced many initial successes. Under the care of the specialists, Patricia and Todd managed to get the *becoming* pregnant thing down pretty good. It was the *staying* pregnant that they couldn't manage.

One miscarriage followed another, which followed yet another.

It was after their fourth heartbreaking loss that Todd, chin trembling but jaw set, told Patricia enough was enough. He was done. No more fertility treatments. No more shots, no more pills, no more taking her temperature. If they had been meant to have a baby, it would have already happened. He could bear no more loss.

Patricia, weary, pale, and anemic, was too sad to disagree.

But despite all the loss and heartbreak, she and Todd, both blessed with optimistic natures, held to the notion that when the time was right, they would somehow get pregnant on their own. If that happened, they convinced themselves, things would be different, more natural, more meant to be. That was it, they told each other. It was the treatments. They had gotten in a rush. Given time, nature would take its course.

Not so. Without the boost of fertility treatments, Patricia didn't get pregnant again. Over time, babies, a topic that for so long had been worked into every conversation, became something that neither one of them brought up anymore.

Yet here it was, three years past their last fertility treatment, and Patricia was late. Late as in *late*.

Unwilling to be disappointed again, Patricia let three weeks pass before she broke down and opened a leftover home pregnancy test she found behind the towels in the bathroom. There was a time when she'd done so many of these things that she'd had the instructions memorized. This time, since it had been so long since she'd done such a test, Patricia was extra careful to follow the directions correctly.

Positive?

No way. She didn't believe it. She dug the box out of the trash. Expired. Well, of course. That explained it. She was just late. Simply, explainably late. Like thousands of other not pregnant women who were late each month.

Three days later, with sweat on her hands, Patricia tested again. This time, the positive result could not be explained away by an expired test. She'd used a fresh test and had sprung for a name-brand product, not some generic or store brand. The package even boasted an expiration date a good six months away.

When she saw the results, Patricia found it hard to draw enough breath to speak. "Todd," she squeaked. "Honey. Could you come here a minute?"

"Whatcha need?" Todd called from the kitchen, where he was pouring milk on his oatmeal. "Help zipping up?" He hoped that she did.

"Todd," she pleaded, *not* in her please-zip-me-up voice, "I think you better come have a look."

Shoot. That voice meant something else. Bathroom sink was probably stopped up again.

"Just a minute. Lemme get the plunger." Tool in hand, Todd stepped into the bathroom. "Whoa! Is that a . . . ? I mean, that looks like a . . . Patricia! What are you doing with a . . . ?" Todd stopped speaking and stared, as slack-jawed as his breathless wife, at the pink plus sign clearly visible in the center of the little plastic device sitting on the edge of the sink.

"We're pregnant!"

Days later, with Todd in the room, Patricia's status was officially confirmed. "Yes. I do believe you are," said the doctor upon examination. "Not sure how far along. Let's do a sonogram and see. Ready now? Okay. When I squirt this jelly, it's going to feel cold."

Bump-a-bump-a-bump-a-bump. A heartbeat—so soon? Patricia and Todd couldn't make out much of their baby on the screen, but they could certainly hear its tiny heart.

"Is it supposed to be that fast?" Todd could

neither tear his eyes from the monitor nor hide his concern.

"Not to worry, Dad," the doctor said with a grin, not pausing from the job at hand. Over and over he moved the imaging wand around and across Patricia's tummy, pausing at specific intervals so as to gauge the fetus's growth and development. "Your baby's heart is beating just as it should. Everything else looks good too. I'm thinking, Patricia, that you're about ten weeks into your pregnancy. Let's see. That would make you due close to Valentine's Day. Uh-huh, I'd say about the fifteenth of February." He turned off the machine, handed Patricia a tissue, and helped her sit up. "Any questions? All right. Before you leave, my nurse has a video to show you and some information I want you both to take home and read. Congratulations. See you in a month."

At home, munching a take-out dinner in front of the TV, Todd said, "See! I knew all along that if we gave ourselves some time, we would have a baby." (He had never been one to refrain from an I-told-you-so.)

Patricia cut him some slack. "Oh, shush," she giggled. "Hand me the TV controller, will you? I'm pregnant. I have to take it easy. And while you're up, could you make me a cup of tea? With a ring of lemon? Thank you, dear." She smiled at him and swatted his bottom as he walked by.

One month later, Patricia stood as lightly as she could on the scale in the doctor's exam room.

"Hmm. Five pounds," he said. "That's a little bit much for this early in your pregnancy. Let's think about cutting back a bit on meals and snacks."

Patricia tried to suck her still-flat stomach in.

"Told you!" teased Todd at her side. "She's been eating ice cream every night before bed. Claims it's to get the calcium. 'Cookies and Cream?' I say. Skim milk will do the same thing, won't it, Doc?"

The doctor winked. "Sweetie, it's okay to eat ice cream. But we also want you to have plenty of good, nutritious food. Another thing—it's true that you're eating for two. But just remember," he said as he held his thumb and forefinger apart. "One of you is very, very tiny. He does not eat much!"

Chagrined, Patricia climbed up onto the table and lay back.

"Blood pressure's good," said the doctor. "Don't see any swelling in your feet." He studied her chart. "No sugar in your urine. Good, good. Now let's take a listen at this critter's little ticker." He lifted Patricia's shirt and placed the listening device on her tummy.

No sound.

"Hiding out, are you? Let's try over here." He moved the device over a bit.

Still no sound.

Patricia and Todd watched while he tested to make sure the machine was working properly. They watched him thump on it, adjust a dial, even change the batteries. The thing was working just fine.

The doctor put the device back on her tummy, but this time he didn't speak. Intent on his task, he methodically moved the device from one spot to another. Over, across, up, down, and back again. Over and over and over again. Took a good five minutes.

Save for Patricia's breathing, nothing broke the silence in the room.

Then the doctor stood up and said in a flat voice, "We need to do a sonogram."

But they already knew.

Patricia went into the hospital for a D and C the next morning.

"I'm so sorry," said the doctor.

"So very sorry," said the nurses.

That night, Patricia dreamed she was in a snow-storm. She saw the faces of her five lost little babies. As she trudged through deep drifts, no matter how hard she tried, she couldn't get to them.

For several weeks, Patricia and Todd intermittently mourned and questioned and cried. But finally, as before, the two of them settled down into their prepregnancy routine. It did not take long for all talk of babies to come to a stop.

• • •

In March of last year, the Scutters moved to Ella Louise. Todd was hired by the city to be the new animal control officer. He's good with animals and good with kids, which is great since problems with the two often run together.

Patricia, an attorney, opened an office just down from the Grace Street church. Ella Louise had never had a female attorney before Patricia, so some people didn't know what to think. But when citizens figured out that Patricia was not, as was initially rumored and feared, one of those rabid, bra-burning feminists, they concluded that she would be an asset to the community. When folks around town met her, they found the new attorney to be a gentle-voiced little thing with freckles and straight, sandy hair that constantly fell in her eyes.

Ella Louise had been without a lawyer for more than ten years. Those who had needed legal help had to travel at least forty-five minutes to get it. For many, this was a hardship. Within weeks of moving into her new office, Patricia's appointment book filled up.

It was a good thing Patricia had never settled on one particular area of law to practice, because every day she found herself tackling a wide variety of legal problems. The folks of Ella Louise needed all kinds of legal help. There were wills to write, transfers of property to be accomplished, traffic tickets to contest, and also divorces, child support, and rowdy teenagers who landed in jail.

Even the occasional adoption.

"Have you and Todd ever thought about it?" asked Sugar Fry. She was Patricia's secretary and one of the first people to make friends with Patricia after she and Todd moved to Ella Louise.

"Thought about what?" They were eating lunch, and Sugar had caught Patricia with a mouth full of ham sandwich.

"Adoption. You know. A baby. Or an older child."

"Not really. If we did adopt, I'd want a newborn, and the chances of getting one are terrible. Remember the Osgoods? That adoption we did early in the spring? It took them three years to get that baby. Mrs. Osgood told me that during the course of those years, two adoptions fell through. By the time the birth mothers told them that they had changed their minds, she and her husband had already fixed the baby's room up —bought toys, clothes, formula, and everything. It was wrenching for them." She wiped her mouth. "Sugar, I have already done wrenching. I don't plan to do it again."

"I know, and I don't blame you after all you've been through. But think about it. In the end, they did get a child. Remember how the three of them looked when it was finally done? Like a family. A real family. I bet they would do it again in a heartbeat."

Patricia didn't answer. What Sugar said was true. She took another bite of her sandwich.

"What about a foreign baby? I hear there are lots of overseas babies, girls especially, who need good homes."

"I don't know. . . . Todd and I wanted children so badly for so long. When it didn't happen, we sort of resigned ourselves to not having any. And you know, after all this time, it really is okay. We have a good life."

"Not that I mean to get in your business," fibbed Sugar, "but you would make such a good mother—and Todd a wonderful father. It's a crying shame that you two don't have a house full of kids."

"Maybe so. But we don't."

Sugar had gone too far. Signaling that the conversation was over, Patricia stood up and brushed sandwich crumbs from her skirt. "What've we got going this afternoon? Is the book full? Wouldn't hurt my feelings to get out of here a little early this evening. How about you?"

That night as she lay spooned in Todd's arms, Patricia replayed the noontime conversation in her mind. Though she'd brushed Sugar's words off at the time, now, in the quiet and the dark, they swirled around and around in her mind.

"Been a long time since we talked about babies, hasn't it?" she whispered. "Do you think about them? Ever? About the children that we would have had?"

"You're not . . . ?" Todd tensed.

"No. No. I'm not."

"Good. I mean . . . It's not that I . . . It's just that . . ."

"Shush. Me too. If I've ever been sure of anything in my life, it's that I don't ever want to be pregnant again." Patricia lost her voice for a moment. "But I've never stopped wishing we had kids."

She turned to face Todd. They lay curled on their sides, knees touching knees. "I'm sorry that it didn't work out," Todd said.

"I know." She reached for a tissue to blow her nose. "There's something we've never talked about, and I'm not sure why. How come we never looked into adopting a baby?"

"You think we could?"

"I don't know."

"You want to?"

"Maybe. I think that I'd at least like to think about it."

That night, both Patricia and Todd fell asleep doing just that.

Six months later, Patricia and Todd's secret plan was the talk of the town.

"I heard they're going to Mexico to get a baby," said Millard Fry.

"Not Mexico. Honduras. It's in Central America. South of Mexico," explained his wife, Sugar.

"I know where it is. How come such a faraway place?"

"God's will," she said. "No other way to explain it. See, they've got some missionary friends living down there who've been helping this young woman. Woman's husband died a few months back, and she's due to have a baby in December. Poor thing's got four children already that she can't afford to feed. When they found out she wanted to find a family who could take care of her baby, the missionaries contacted the Scutters."

"And they were looking for a baby?" asked Millard.

"Let's just say they were open to the idea," said Sugar.

"Sad for the mother, but what a lucky little baby," said Millard, who liked Patricia and Todd a lot.

"A blessing for them all. But don't tell anyone. No one knows that they're doing this."

But, of course, in a small town like Ella Louise, things don't stay a secret for long. At the Chamber of Commerce, Mayor Tinker asked his assistant, Faye Beth Newman, what she knew.

"Don't tell anyone, but I heard that the baby's

due the first week of December. Patricia and Todd are supposed to fly down a little while later just in case she goes past due. Todd's never flown. Said he never would. But that was before this baby came into the picture." Faye Beth winked. "From what I hear, one of Patricia's friends from law school has prepared all of the paperwork. Says they should be able to bring the baby home without a hitch."

"Bless those kids' hearts." Mayor Tinker teared up. "Do they know if they're getting a boy or a girl?"

"No idea."

"I doubt that they care."

At a gathering of the Gentle Thimble Quilting Club, Bessie Bishop, this year's president, called the meeting to order and moved that the club's next project be a baby quilt for the Scutter's little one.

"I second the motion," said Esther Vaughn.

The motion passed. Everyone agreed that they would have to work quickly in order to have the quilt ready for the surprise baby shower that the ladies of Grace Street Church planned to give.

Rochelle Shartle, too excited to care that the baby was supposed to be a secret, called Patricia right up. "Congratulations! Rocky and I are so happy for you! I want to give the baby a 'Welcome to Ella Louise' party as soon as you get home. Everyone who's come to the café in the past week has said that we ought to do something to welcome that little baby. We'll have the party here at the Wild Flour, of course. Melissa and I'll make punch and coffee and coconut cake. 'Course, I need to know what day you'll be back so I can have it all ready."

Patricia was touched. As soon as she got off the phone, she gave Sugar the news. "Wonder how word got out that Todd and I were even getting a baby?" she asked.

"Beats me," Sugar said.

Patricia wasn't even mad.

While the entire town of Ella Louise was terribly excited about the coming baby, Todd's generally agreeable seventy-seven-year-old mother voiced surprising unease. "Honduras? Where's that?" she asked in a long-distance telephone call.

"Central America, Mom."

"Where?"

"Close to Mexico. Down south."

She fell silent.

"Mom? You there?"

"Son, there's lots of babies right here that need good homes. Why, they had some orphan children on the 10:00 news last night that were looking for families. I don't see any need for you kids to be going so far off when you can get yourselves a regular American baby."

"Mom, there's more to it than that. This baby

needs a home too. We can give it a good one. Besides, once we adopt the baby, it will be an American."

"A little Mexican," Todd heard his mother mutter to herself. "Will it have brown eyes?"

"Most likely."

"Brown hair too?"

"I expect so."

Brown hair, brown eyes. Likely the baby would have brown skin too.

"Mom, we want you to be happy for us."

"I am. I mean, I will be. But Todd, there's some things about this that worry me."

Todd knew from experience that it was best not to argue with his mother. "We're bringing the baby home on Tuesday the twelfth. Our flight arrives right at noon. How about the three of us swing by and pick you up on our way back to Ella Louise? Folks in town are giving us a big party. It'll be fun. You can stay with us a few days, get to know your new grandchild."

Though she was still not convinced, Todd got her to agree.

"Mom's getting older. More set in her ways," Todd told Patricia when he hung up. "She's worried about us getting a baby from way off. Thinks we should get an American baby."

"You mean a white baby?"

"She didn't come out and say it, but I think that's pretty much what she means."

81

"Don't worry. Much as she loves kids, once she sees the baby, she'll come around."

"I hope so."

And when, two weeks later, Todd knocked on his mother's door, it was clear that she had. "Come in this house! I've been looking for you for hours! Where's Patricia?"

Patricia stood on the steps behind Todd, out of his mother's line of vision. Todd stepped aside.

"Did you get the baby? There she is! A girl? Let me see her! Oh my goodness, give her to me." She took the baby from Patricia and gently lifted the blanket from her new granddaughter's face. "Look." Tears filled her eyes. "Isn't she just the prettiest little thing."

Not taking her eyes off the baby, she directed them inside. "You all come in. Sit down. Patricia, go on in the kitchen and fix you and Todd something to drink. I'm going to sit right here and hold this baby."

Todd went in to help Patricia. He noticed a box with a California return address sitting on the kitchen table. "What's this, Mom?" he called to her. "This big box. You order something?" Except for Lillian Vernon, who she considered a long-distance friend, his mother didn't trust folks who sold stuff through the mail.

His mother came into the kitchen, still carrying the baby. "That's my Spanish lessons," she said.

"You're studying Spanish?"

" 'Course I am. Aren't you?"

"Uh, no. I'm not."

"Well, when do you intend to start? You don't have more than a few months—a year at the most."

"A few months? A year?" Todd was confused. "What are you talking about? Mom, why would I want to learn Spanish?"

"Son! How else do you intend to be able to talk to your daughter?" she huffed. "Now, I admit, when you first told me you were getting a little Mexican baby . . ."

"Honduran," Todd interrupted.

She waved him quiet. "I was afraid that I couldn't do it—that learning a new language would be too hard. Fact is, I didn't know where to start or how to go about it. You forget, Todd, that I'm an old woman. It's not so easy for me to learn new things. But then I saw where you could order these Spanish lessons from off of the TV. The lessons came yesterday, and I stayed up till 10:00 last night listening to a tape and filling out my workbook. Not to be bragging or anything, but I've learned five Spanish words already. Did you know that *abuela* means grandmother?"

Todd struggled to keep the grin off his face. Careful not to squish the baby, he gathered his mother into his arms. "I love you, Mom."

"I love you too. Watch her little head now."

• • •

Todd and Patricia's baby, Alecia, is now ten months. She's a chubby-cheeked, brown-eyed little darling who's crazy about her grandma. She kicks her little legs and breaks into a grin whenever she sees her, which is often these days.

"*Te amo*," says Grandma to Alecia.

"Goo," says Alecia.

"See," Grandma says to Todd. "She understands."

Without a doubt.

6

Angel Incognito

Four pairs of shorts. Two pairs of jeans.

Ten T-shirts. Two long-sleeve shirts.

Flashlight.

Rain poncho.

One pair of athletic shoes. One pair of hiking boots.

Underwear for a week and a half.

Bible. Notebook. Pens.

Sarah Strickland, mother of twelve-year-old twins Kevin and Josh, struggled to fit all of the items printed on the camp-provided "What to Pack" list into her boys' two suitcases.

Sarah's sneaky sons, drafted into perching their bony bottoms on the bags while she snapped the latches, watched her doings and silently noted that there was precious little room left for them to squeeze in the contraband that their friends had assured them was essential—important stuff like water balloons, bubble gum, whoopee cushions, and fake vomit.

"There. You're all set," their mother said. "We'll pack your toothbrushes in the morning. I think they'll fit in the side zipper pocket. Can you guys think of anything else?"

They could not.

Kevin and Josh waited till their mother left the room and they could hear her running her evening bath. Then they rearranged. Taking out a few unnecessary items like half of the underwear and socks, which they hid under Josh's bed, they were able to shove almost all of the essentials in. Only the fake vomit refused to fit, but that was no problem. Josh could stuff it down his shirt, which was probably a good idea anyway. He didn't want it to get torn up.

"Wait, Kev, where's my joke book?" remembered Josh. They'd discussed bringing it and had agreed that the treasured, dog-eared volume of classic bathroom humor would make for some great late-night, laugh-till-you-pass-gas reading.

"It's packed. I put it in the side pocket of the green bag," said Kevin.

"Good. Did you zip it up so Mom won't find it?"

"Yeah. I did."

Kevin and Josh really wanted to ride the church bus to Camp Road Runner. Some of their friends were doing so, and camp personnel had arranged to meet the bus when it arrived. But their mom, Sarah, who they had begged and cajoled into letting them sign up for their first stay at a ten-day session of church sleep-away camp, insisted on driving them the two hours south.

Once there, she was not about to let them out near the gate with the other kids. Oh no. Not their mother. She insisted on escorting them to their cabin, meeting their counselor, shaking his hand, and finding out stuff about him. He turned out to be a bearded Christian college junior, a physical education major. Dressed to impress, he was wearing faded army fatigues cut off below the knees, flip-flops, and a yellow T-shirt that read "Follow Me to the Library."

Sarah did not believe she had ever seen anyone with such hairy feet.

"Pancho Jones." He gave each of the boys a high five. "Hey, Kev. Yo, Josh. Welcome to Camp Road Runner. Come on in and pick yourselves out a bunk. Nice to meet you, Miz Strickland."

Sarah wondered how well the camp screened the staff.

Stalling, Sarah decided to help her sons make up their beds. "Mom!" protested Kevin in a desperate whisper. "I don't need any help. I can put the sheet on by myself!"

Then she proceeded to give Pancho detailed instructions on how to give the boys their vitamins. "One of these twice a day, two of these once a day, and three each of these every other day. Understand?"

Pancho wrote it all down.

Kevin and Josh walked their mom down the

hill to the parking area and told her their good-byes at the side of the van, looking around to make sure the guys couldn't see their mom kiss them.

"Wear deodorant every day, and don't forget to write!" In their bags, Sarah had packed six stamped envelopes addressed to Ella Louise.

Finally, she was ready to leave. "Bye, boys! Have a great time," she said through tears.

As soon as she was gone, Kevin and Josh raced back up the hill to where Pancho and their five cabin mates were hanging out. It was pretty quiet inside the cabin. Not much happened the first afternoon of camp, and everyone acted pretty bored. The boys, most of them away from home for the first time like Josh and Kevin, were feeling a wee bit homesick already. They were all either sitting slump-shouldered on the edges of their bunks or lying down, staring at the rafters over-head.

Not Kevin and Josh. Emboldened as always by the presence of each other, they were eager to have fun.

"Pancho, what do we do now?" asked Kevin.

"Can we go swimming?" asked Josh.

"Can we go down to the creek?" asked Kevin.

Hearing the twins' questions, cabin mates Lindon, James, Rudy, Carl, and Max's ears all perked up.

"Yeah, Pancho. Can we?"

Pancho looked at his watch. "Guys, I know everybody's tired of just hanging out here. We'll get moving really soon. But for now we've gotta stay close to our cabin 'cause there's two more campers coming." He looked at his list. "Trey Biddles and Ralph Smart. Both of 'em from Oklahoma. Soon as they get here and we get 'em settled in, we'll do something. Promise. In the meantime, come 'ere." He led them outside and pointed to a cleared area fifty yards away from the cabin. "See the basket nailed up on that pine tree? Halfway down the hill? Y'all can go down there and shoot some hoops if you want. Just don't go any farther than that."

The boys ran down to the hoop and shot around just long enough to begin arguing and raising dust when Kevin stopped play by holding the ball.

"Hey! What're you doin'?" red-faced Rudy asked.

Kevin motioned toward the cabin. "Looks like the last two guys just got here. Let's go see."

"Only one of 'em's here," argued Rudy. "That other guy's too big. He's gotta be the dad. Come on. Let's play ball."

Rudy was proved wrong when Pancho called them to the cabin. They raced each other back.

"Dudes," Pancho said to the sweaty group, "this is Trey and this is Ralph. They're our last two campers. Make 'em feel welcome. Tell 'em who you are."

The boys said nothing. They just stood there, slack-jawed and staring.

"Hey, there," the first guy said, sticking out his hand. "I'm Ralph."

This guy was big, as big as a grown-up. Shoot. He *was* a grown-up. Wasn't this supposed to be a camp for kids?

Then the other guy said, "Hello. I'm Trey. What's your name?"

He was . . .

He was . . .

Uh . . .

The other guy? The last kid to move into the cabin?

He was mentally handicapped. Twelve years old, but with Down's Syndrome. A mentally handicapped kid at Camp Road Runner. They allowed that? Since when?

Truth was, from the first time he'd heard about it, Trey had wanted to come to camp. All the other kids at his church got to go to camp. He was twelve now. Wasn't that how old you had to be?

When Ralph, Trey's twenty-eight-year-old youth director, heard how much Trey wanted to go to camp, he saw no reason why Trey should have to stay home. Sure, he would need a little extra help, but that was no big deal. After discussing the idea with Trey's mother, Ralph decided that this year Trey would get to go to camp—and he would go too. They would stay in the same cabin and be bunkmates and buddies, and when Trey needed help, he would give it. When he didn't, he wouldn't. They would both be just two of the guys.

Right.

Josh and Kevin and the rest of the boys stood looking at their feet.

Finally, Pancho punched Carl in the arm. "Whatsa matter, guys? Be polite. Introduce yourselves."

"Okay. I'm Carl."

"I'm Rudy."

"Hey. I'm Lindon."

"James."

"Max."

"Josh."

"Kevin." Kevin shook Trey's hand. No one else moved.

Pancho ended the awkward moment and got things moving. "Men, we've got an hour before dinner. Then we'll have worship with the rest of the camp, and after that, it's Roadrunner silly song time. Now'd be a good time to take a hike around camp. Everybody ready?"

The boys waited on the porch of the cabin, still not saying much, while Lindon went inside to change his shoes.

It was James, chewing on a blade of grass, who

saw Maggie first. She was trotting her way toward the cabin.

"Whose dog?" he asked.

"Dog?" said Lindon.

"Here, girl," called Max.

Maggie came over. She sniffed the feet of each boy in turn.

"Does she bite?" asked Ralph.

"Naw. I don't think so," said Pancho. "She hasn't yet."

"Where'd she come from?"

"She's the official camp dog, aren't you, girl," said Pancho, scratching Maggie's ears.

No one knew where Maggie had come from. A pooch of indeterminable heritage, Maggie had wandered up before the start of camp and had made herself right at home. The staff, there for a week of training before the arrival of the first set of summer campers, fed her, petted her, and fixed a dry place for her to sleep under the roof of the facility's open-air pavilion.

The camp director liked Maggie and believed that having a dog around would help discourage snakes. The campers would enjoy her too. As soon as it was clear that no one was going to claim her and that she had decided to stay around, the director coaxed her into the cab of his pickup truck and drove her into town to the vet so she could get her shots. Once she was pronounced fit, he brought her back to camp, and there she seemed content to stay. And no wonder. Camp Road Runner occupied a good forty acres. With squirrels to chase, a creek to drink from, and a hundred kids around all the time, Camp Road Runner was about as close to heaven as a dog could get. And since she was such a well-behaved dog, there was no problem allowing Maggie the run of the place.

Once she'd made the rounds of all the boys in Pancho's cabin, and made herself acquainted with each of their smells, she walked over to Trey and sat down at his feet. Trey dropped to one knee. "Hi there. You sure are a pretty dog." He petted her head and then ran his hands along her back. Maggie lay down, then rolled over so he could rub her tummy.

"Trey, I believe you've made yourself a friend," said Pancho. "Everybody ready now? Let's go."

That night at the staff meeting, Trey was discussed.

"Pancho, how are the other campers in your cabin treating him?" the director asked.

"Okay, I guess. They aren't making fun of him or anything."

"Guess that's about as good as we can hope for. I want Trey to have a good time, but I also don't want him to slow your other boys down. They deserve to get what they came for. If you have any problems, let me know."

The next morning, when Pancho's boys stepped

out of their cabin, they found Maggie asleep on the porch. She had been there all night. "Hi, girl. Whatcha doing?" She raised her head and let all the boys pet her, even licked Kevin's and Josh's hands, but it was Trey that she fell in behind when the boys trooped to the flag pole for the morning devotional.

It was also Trey whom Maggie waited for outside the dining hall, and Trey whom she sat beside while he painted a wooden birdhouse during craft time.

"Maggie sure likes you," said Max.

"I like her too," said Trey. The sound of Trey's voice made Maggie raise her head.

"Dog's crazy about Trey," observed Pancho.

"I know it," said Ralph.

"Does he have a dog at home?"

"Nope. His mom's allergic."

That night while Pancho was at his staff meeting, the boys heard Maggie whining at the screen door of the cabin. "Can we let her in?" they asked Ralph.

"I don't see what it would hurt. Go ahead," said Ralph.

Lindon got up and opened the door. Maggie scooted in, sniffed around just a bit, and then hopped right up onto Trey's bed. Trey was already asleep. Maggie didn't disturb him but gingerly curled up around his feet, put her head on her paws, and let out a contented sigh.

"She sure likes Trey," said Lindon, who wished that Maggie had wanted to sleep on his bed.

"She likes our cabin best," said Josh.

"Yeah. But she likes Trey best of all of us."

"He's her favorite."

And he was. Maggie followed Trey around like a . . . well, like a dog. When he spoke, she perked up her ears and listened to his every word. When he pet her, she quivered with pleasure. And when he called her to come into the lake for a swim she plunged right in, though she hated getting her feet wet. Of course, it was next to Trey that she stood and shook herself dry once they got out of the lake.

Trey didn't mind.

Maggie's affection made camp easier for Trey. The kids were treating him all right, but it was nice that when he fell behind on a hike, she slowed down too. He didn't feel as bad when he was puzzled by one of Josh's jokes, because she didn't look like she understood either. It was great that when he wanted to dig and make roads in the dirt instead of playing basketball, she kept him company in the shade. And when Trey fell asleep during the group Bible study, Maggie nodded off too.

Maggie also made Trey's stay at camp easier for Pancho. The two were such good buddies that Pancho didn't have to worry about Trey feeling left out. While the guys in the cabin didn't treat

Trey bad or anything, they didn't try very hard to include him in stuff either.

On the afternoon of the fifth day of the ten-day session, Doc, the camp's horse wrangler, unwisely decided to lead Pancho and his boys on a new trail. "You fellows up to it?" Doc asked. "The horses aren't as used to it as the other trail. Some of 'em might balk a bit. You'll have to make 'em mind if they start to head back to the corral and the barn before it's time."

Well, of course they were up to it, though they were all, except for Carl, who lived on a cattle ranch, at least a little bit afraid of the group of aged, gentle camp steeds. They wouldn't have admitted to that for anything, though.

"Ready?" Doc asked. "Everybody got their reins? Got your feet in the stirrups? All right. Fall in line."

So they did. First Doc, then Carl, Max, Lindon, and James, then Rudy, Kevin, and Josh. Trey and Ralph, riding double, brought up the rear. Maggie, of course, trotted at Trey's horse's heels.

The trail didn't appear to be anything special. No big rocks in the way. No fallen trees to jump over. Not even a creek to cross. What was the big deal?

Not much, except that the horses, cranky in the face of change, trudged along with their ears back, pausing every few yards to snatch mouthfuls of tall growing weeds. This made for slow going with lots of stops and starts.

"Pull on the reins, fellas," called Doc from up ahead. "And give 'em just a little kick. That's it. They'll go if you show 'em who's boss."

After Doc gave his instructions, Ralph and Trey's horse—the gentlest, slowest of the bunch—suddenly took to stomping, kicking, and carrying on.

"Whoa!" Trey yelled, holding on to Ralph with both hands. "Whoa!"

"Ralph, pull back on the reins!" hollered Doc from up ahead. "Pull back on the reins!"

It could have been that Trey's heel, in spite of Doc's careful instructions, had landed too far back into his horse's ticklish flanks. Or maybe the horse got stung by a bee or a horsefly. Regardless of whatever caused the horse to pitch such a fit, Ralph could not get control. Trey tumbled right off the horse and into the weeds.

"Trey, are you all right?" Doc was there in an instant, kneeling over him.

"Trey, are you hurt?" Ralph too was off the horse.

Though he was shook up, Trey was fine. He had been wearing a helmet when he fell. His hands were bloodied and skinned from breaking his fall, but other than that, he wasn't hurt.

"You sure you're okay, buddy?" asked Ralph.

"Can you sit up?" asked Doc. To the other boys,

he called, "He's all right. You guys stay on your horses. It's okay to let 'em eat, but don't get off the trail."

Trey wiped his nose on the tail of his shirt. "I don't think I want to ride any more."

"No problem." Ralph gave him a hug. "You and me'll walk down. We'll just lead our horse. That be okay?"

"Uh-huh. Where's Maggie?"

"I dunno," said Doc. "She's here somewhere. Probably off chasing a squirrel or something. Maaaggie, Maaaggie, here girl!"

She didn't come.

Doc called her again. Ralph too.

Still no Maggie.

"Hold on a second." Pancho spotted fur in a low spot off to the side of the trail. "I think I see her. Looks like she's hurt."

Doc and Ralph helped Trey to his feet. When the three of them got to where the dog was, they couldn't believe it. Maggie lay very, very still.

Ralph held Trey back. Doc bent to check. "Guys, I can't believe it, but she's dead."

"How? What happened?"

"I don't know. Best I can guess, horse must've kicked her in the head."

Trey began to sob. Ralph held him close.

Back at the cabin, Trey lay on his bunk with his pillow covering his head. He didn't move. He refused to eat supper, and even skipped swim time, which he loved. "You guys go on. Trey'll be all right," Pancho said, shooing the rest of the boys out of the cabin. When they were gone, he whispered to Ralph, "He's pretty upset. You think we should call his mother?"

"Not yet." It was 9:00 by then and Trey had gone to sleep. "Let's see how he is in the morning. I'll sit up tonight in case he wakes up crying or needing something."

"You sure?"

"Yeah. I'm not that tired, and I can sleep in the morning."

But at 1:30 Ralph fell asleep, in spite of his best efforts. It was Kevin who woke up and heard Trey sniffling. Not sure what to do, Kevin woke up Josh, who woke up Carl, who woke up everybody else—except for Pancho and Ralph. The boys slid out of their bunks and stood in a huddle on the cabin's concrete floor, shifting and shivering in their boxers and T-shirts.

"Trey's crying," Kevin whispered. "We gotta do something."

"What?" asked Josh.

"I dunno. Talk to him or something."

"Trey? You all right?" Josh spoke to Trey's back.

"We're sorry about Maggie," said Rudy.

"Yeah. She was a really good dog," said Max.

"When my dog got hit by a car, I cried for a week," said Lindon.

"You did?" Trey rolled over and faced the seven.

"I cried for a month when my dog died," offered Carl.

"I cried for three months when my cat died," topped Rudy.

No one knew what to say next.

"Man, I'm hungry," said Kevin. "Anybody got anything to eat?"

"I do. I've got Pringles and M&Ms," said Lindon. "I'm starving too."

"Me too. I've got some jerky," said Max.

Just then Ralph rolled over and Pancho's snoring stopped. "Shhh! Keep it down," hissed Josh. "We'll get in trouble if anybody finds out we've got food. Let's go to the bathhouse. Nobody'll catch us there. Everybody grab what you've got and let's go."

"Come on, Trey." Kevin helped Trey slide out of his bunk. "Where's your shoes? Careful now. Do your hands hurt?"

"Just when I move 'em."

"Stick your foot up here and let me tie."

"Thanks, Kevin."

"No problem. Ready?"

The next morning, when Ralph realized that he'd drifted off, he felt really bad. He told Pancho that he feared Trey might have cried during the night. "Trey? Time to wake up. You sleep okay, buddy?"

Trey didn't want to wake up.

But, then again, neither did Josh, Kevin, Rudy, Carl, James, Max, or Lindon. The whole cabin acted like they were worn out.

"What's up with you men?" teased Pancho. "If I didn't know better, I'd think that y'all had been up all night running around the camp or something."

Sixteen bare feet hit the gritty cabin floor. "We're up," said Kevin.

"Yeah, we're up, Pancho," the rest agreed, suddenly intent on looking wide awake.

Pancho looked over at Ralph and shrugged. "Whatever. Flagpole devo in ten. Let's not be the last cabin there."

When he stepped out of the cabin, Trey must've remembered that Maggie was gone, because he looked like he was about to cry. Max, who had walked out with Trey, threw his arm across Trey's shoulders. "Come on. It'll be all right. You ready? We don't have to wait on those guys."

The others, minutes later on their way down the hill to the flag, discussed a plan of action amongst themselves. "Man, he lost his best friend," Lindon said.

"Trey was crazy about that dog," Josh agreed.

"We gotta keep him company so he don't feel so bad," Carl said.

And so they did their best.

That afternoon, Max played in the dirt with

Trey while the other guys shot hoops. They made roads and bridges and tunnels and stuff.

Josh and Kevin sat by Trey at lunch and listened to him tell knock-knock jokes. Some of the ones he told were funnier than the ones printed in their book. "We gotta write that one down," said Josh. "Trey, you want me to open up your milk?"

Their efforts, though well meant, weren't enough. Trey was still sad.

"We should have a funeral for Maggie," Lindon suggested.

"You mean with prayers and preaching and stuff?" James asked.

"We can't. It's too late. I heard Pancho tell Ralph that the staff buried Maggie behind Craft Hall last night," Carl said. "You can't have a funeral without a body." Having recently lost a great-uncle, Carl was knowledgeable about such things.

"It could be a memorial service then," Lindon said.

Memorial service. You didn't have to have a body for one of those. The cabin agreed that Lindon had a good plan. And despite day-long whispered preparations, the boys managed to keep the service a secret until sunset.

"Don't ask any questions. Please. Just come with us," the boys said to Pancho and Ralph. "Trey, come on. We've got something to show you. Up the hill. Behind Craft Hall."

"But that's where they . . ."

"Come on, Trey." Josh and Kevin took him by the hands.

"Quiet please. Gather 'round," said Lindon when they arrived at Maggie's grave. He removed his cap. The other guys took theirs off too. "Maggie was a good dog." He coughed. "She was Trey's special friend. We're gonna miss her."

Carl had made a cross for Maggie's grave out of two whittled sticks and a leather lace from one of his hiking boots. Reverently, he stuck it in the ground at the northernmost end of Maggie's grave. Josh and Kevin had gathered enough smooth stones from the creekbed to surround the mound of her grave. When Lindon gave them the signal, they pulled the stones from their pockets and placed them all around. Max had picked a big bunch of wildflowers. When the stones were in place, he pulled out the bunch from under his shirt and placed it on her grave.

James read Psalm twenty-three, and Rudy said a dismissal prayer. Everyone raised their head. At first, no one seemed to know what to say or do next.

It was Josh, finally, who broke the silent, solemn spell. "Amen."

"Amen," said the rest in unison.

"Last one to the cabin's a rotten egg!"

"Come on, Trey!"

"Trey, wait for me!"

As Pancho and Ralph stood back and watched the boys urge slow-moving Trey along, as they saw Max catch him when he stumbled and Carl bend to tie his shoe, as they took note of the entire rowdy bunch stalling so that Trey wouldn't come in last, they concluded that Josh was wrong. There wasn't a rotten egg in the bunch.

While Maggie had been Trey's first camp friend, she was not his last.

I am a spiritual person. I believe in God and Jesus, in heaven and in grace. I believe in angels too, though there's a lot about them that I don't understand.

What do they look like?

Do they have halos and wings?

Do they all play gold harps?

The Bible, in Hebrews 13:2, says "Do not forget to entertain strangers, for by so doing some people have entertained angels without knowing it."

They appear incognito?

Now that's a thought.

Can you imagine a better disguise for an angel to don than scruffy brown fur and a cold, wet nose?

Not me.

7

Millard and Millie

Millard and Sugar Fry moved from Chicago to Ella Louise in the fall of 1958, soon after they got married.

Having lived all of their lives north of the Mason-Dixon line, the Frys, especially Sugar, wondered how they, a black couple, would be accepted in a small Southern town.

"You think we'll have any friends?" asked Sugar. "Are there any other people like us living there?"

"I don't know," Millard said optimistically. "Might be a few. Now Sugar, it'll take a while, but we'll be all right. Don't worry about it. We've got each other. What more could we need?" He pulled Sugar to him and plopped a kiss on her cheek.

Sugar, who was leaving behind her two big sisters, her mother, and her best friend since third grade, kept her thoughts to herself. However, she could think of a lot more things than just Millard that she needed. A man is a good thing to have, but women need friends. It's in their natures, her grandmother had always said.

"Long as we work hard, we'll be fine," Millard assured her. Millard, a carpenter and handyman, was not afraid of hard work.

"We'll make us a good life, baby. You'll see."

And though it took them almost a year to get used to Southern ways, as well as Southern foods ("Okra? What do I do with it?" asked Sugar the first time Millard brought home a sack of the fuzzy green stuff), Millard and Sugar were quite happy in Ella Louise. He found plenty of work, and the two of them became good friends with another newlywed and new-to-the-community couple, Alfred and Tiny Tinker. The fact that Millard and Sugar were black, Alfred and Tiny white, mattered not a whit.

Within a year of moving to Ella Louise, Sugar gave birth to a sweet little baby girl, whom Millard named Shonda. He was wild with plans and with pride.

"She's gonna have the best of everything," he proclaimed. "Books, pretty dresses, and music lessons. I'll see to it." And he worked even harder than before.

As Shonda grew up and blossomed into a lovely young lady, one who caught the eyes of young men, Millard began to fret. "Shonda, don't even be thinking about boys. You're going to college. And you're going to do good. You've got to keep your head in your books. Understand?"

"Yes, Daddy."

"Me and your mother never had the chance to go to college."

"I know, Daddy." Shonda had heard this lecture about a million times before.

Millard's obsessive determination that Shonda get an education provides explanation as to why he was so upset when the disturbing word got back to him. Someone had seen his baby girl, by now a university student, sitting in a Chevy pickup at the Sonic Drive-in, necking with some boy. At 2:00 in the afternoon!

Now, it is joked in Ella Louise that if a person hasn't heard a rumor by noon, it's that person's civic duty to start one. So Millard figured the story to be nothing more than a silly town rumor. Hadn't he raised Shonda better than that? Of course he had! Still, on the off chance that there was even a shred of truth to the tale, he thought it best to have a little daddy-daughter talk with his girl.

"Sugar, get on the phone and tell Shonda that she needs to come home this weekend. I want to talk to her."

But Sugar wasn't able to reach Shonda.

"What do you mean, not in? Ten o'clock on a Tuesday night? Well, then leave a message at the dorm. Tell her to call home as soon as she comes in."

When Shonda didn't call back for three days, Millard fumed. When she finally did call, she spoke to the answering machine. "Sorry Mama and Daddy. Can't come home this weekend. Lots to do. Maybe I'll make it in another week or so."

"She probably has a test to study for," Sugar said, trying to soothe Millard. "Honey, it's her junior year. She's got more on her mind. She's not our baby anymore, and we can't be ordering her around like she is."

Millard did not see why not.

On the weekend that Shonda finally did come home from school, which was an hour's drive away, she did everything she could to avoid being alone with her daddy. On Friday night, she went with her mother to buy groceries. After that, they went to Wal-Mart, where they stayed until after 10:00. Millard got to yawning so bad that he finally gave up and went to bed. On Saturday, Shonda didn't get up until Millard had already gone to work. That night, she stayed holed up in the bathroom for what seemed like forever. When she came out, she said she had a headache and went up to her room. Not until Sunday did Millard find time to have a word with her.

"Come sit with me on the porch, honey. Let's talk." He patted the spot on the swing next to him. "How's school?"

"Good, Daddy. Really good."

"You like your new roommate?"

"Well, she snores and she has to have a light on at night, but other than that, I like her all right." Shonda smiled.

"How about boys? You been talking to any boys?"

"A few." She sat on her hands and unsuccessfully tried to look him in the eye.

"Been out on any dates?"

"Just a couple. Daddy, I'm twenty years old."

"There's time for that later, girl. You know me and your mother expect you to get your degree."

"Daddy, why are you asking me all this? You know I've got lots of friends. Some of them are boys, and yes, sometimes we go out on dates. Everything's fine."

Millard called her bluff. "Jerry Jeff Maffett was traveling through. Says he saw you and some boy in a car at the Sonic. Said he saw you kissing."

Shonda did not blink.

"That true?"

She did not answer.

Millard drew a breath. "Little girl, I raised you better than that. You know I did. I best not be hearing any more of you hanging all over some boy, putting on a show for the whole town. If ever I do, you can kiss college good-bye. I will bring you back home to where me and your mother can look after you. Do I make myself clear?"

He thought he had.

• • •

Two months later, Millard and Sugar got a late-night call. When they heard the ring, they picked up on different phones at the same time.

"Hello?"

"Hello?"

"Mama? Daddy? It's me. I need to come home."

"Tonight? Honey, what's wrong?" Sugar could tell Shonda had been crying. Millard could too.

"I-I-I just want to come home."

"What do you think's the matter?" asked Millard after they'd hung up.

Sugar couldn't guess.

When Shonda pulled up into the driveway well after midnight, she looked a mess—nose runny, skin blotchy, hair in her eyes.

Sugar reached her first. "Honey, come on in the house." Shonda fell into her arms. Millard guided the two of them up the steps.

"What's happened? Are you cold, honey?" Shonda was trembling. "Millard, she needs that afghan off the rocker to put around her shoulders. There now." Sugar tucked the blanket close. "Baby, what is it?"

Shonda wiped her nose with the back of her hand. Millard handed her a clean handkerchief out of his back pocket.

"There was a car wreck. This afternoon." Shonda rocked back and forth.

"Are you hurt?" Millard said sharply.

"No—yes—I mean, it wasn't me. My friend was on his way home from work. They say he ran a red light. I went to the hospital as soon as I heard, but it was too late. I never even got to see him." Her face crumpled. "I thought he would be all right, but he wasn't. They say that he died, but I can't believe he's really gone. I just can't believe that it's real."

Millard gathered his little girl in his arms and breathed a silent, selfish prayer of thanks. It could have been his child killed tonight. Even though she was twenty years old and had been driving for four years, every time he watched Shonda get behind the wheel of a car he worried that it might be the last time he would see her. So many kids have accidents. So many get killed. What agony the family of the young man must be going through right now!

"I'm so sorry, honey." He kissed the top of her head. "You did right coming home. We're so glad you're here. Was the boy someone from around here? Did he have a family?"

"He had me."

Millard stroked her hair. Sugar leaned close.

"You were dating this boy?" asked Millard.

"Yes."

"Were you serious?"

Shonda drew her knees up under her chin, laid her head on her mother's shoulder, and whispered, "We were going to get married. I'm going to have a baby, Mama."

For a long, long time, no one said a word.

Finally, Shonda reached for Millard. "I'm sorry, Daddy. Please don't be mad. I know what we did was wrong. We wanted to get married, but we couldn't figure out how. I tried to tell you, but I couldn't. I'm so sorry, Daddy. I didn't mean for this to happen. Really, I didn't. I know you're disappointed. But please, Daddy, please don't be mad."

Millard didn't respond.

It is hard to speak when one has no wind.

Sugar spoke instead. "Shonda, are you saying that the boy who was killed in the accident tonight was the one who . . ."

"Yes."

"What was his name? Do his folks know about . . . about . . ." Sugar's voice trailed off.

"They don't know."

Millard blew his nose. When he finally spoke, his voice was hard. "Shonda, you have hurt your mother. This is not what we expected of you, and it is not what we wanted for you. You knew better. Things around here will be different from now on. You—well, you have made your bed, young lady. Now you've got to lie in it."

Later that week, when Shonda and Sugar moved Shonda's things out of the dorm and back into her old room, Millard did not offer to help.

When Shonda made his favorite pie, placed it, hot out of the oven, in front of him, Millard offered no thanks. When the two of them met in the hall during late-night trips to the bathroom, Millard looked down and gave her wide berth.

Millard spoke to Shonda only when necessary and never looked her in the eyes. Weeks went by. The bigger Shonda grew, the more Millard let on that he was repulsed by the sight of her.

"Mama, why is Daddy acting like this? I can't take back what's happened," Shonda grieved. "Is he never going to forgive me? And what about when the baby comes? Mama, there is going to be a little child in this house. He can't ignore it."

Sugar, caught in the middle, tried to soften Millard up. "Shonda's not going to finish the semester, Millard. She doesn't think she'd be able to hold up."

"Suit herself." He held the newspaper up in front of his face. Yet he wondered if Shonda was all right. She did look tired. He knew she wasn't sleeping, because he heard her up walking almost every night.

Sugar tried again another day. "Shonda's resting. Her feet are swollen. Dr. Strickland says she needs to stay out of the heat."

"Fine by me." Millard turned on sports. Swollen feet? Was that a serious sign? One of the waitresses at the Wild Flour Café had had something called toxemia a little while back. She nearly died. If he recalled right, it seemed like her trouble started out with swollen feet.

"Shonda's going to the doctor tomorrow. She thinks she'll find out whether the baby's going to be a boy or a girl. Don't you want to come along? You wouldn't have to go in. You could wait out front. It would mean so much to Shonda if you would."

"Sugar, I don't want to hear about it. Do you understand? Shonda is mine and I take care of my own, but she made a choice. She knew how I felt. She threw away her morals. As long as I live, I will never accept any baby born like that as one of my kin."

Sugar pushed harder. "Millard Fry, this little one will be our first grandchild. It didn't ask to be brought into this world. It's a little baby, as innocent as innocent can be. It's not going to have a daddy. Least you can do is be its granddaddy."

Millard laid down the newspaper and looked at the TV.

Sugar tried to hide her concern, but with every passing day, she grew more and more worried. Her Millard was a good man. Better than most. If he could reject his own flesh and blood, she shuddered to think how other people would react to her first grandbaby. Even though unwed motherhood was no longer uncommon, certain

114

tongues were already wagging at the fact that Shonda was pregnant without a husband. Sugar cringed to think about how the community might treat the baby.

As Shonda's delivery date got closer and closer, Sugar, at her wit's end and believing that Shonda's baby would have an easier time of it if she had some kind of edge, took to praying for God to make the baby either pretty or smart. "Lord, give her brains or beauty. Amen."

No one expected Millard to be the one to take Shonda to the hospital. But as it turned out, Sugar was off running errands when, three weeks early and without a single warning contraction, Shonda's water broke. When it happened, Shonda was standing at the sink, rinsing off supper dishes. For a moment, she just stared at the warm puddle between her bare and swollen feet. Then she put her face in the dishrag and started to cry.

Millard, who'd been sitting at the kitchen table, eating a piece of pie, heard her sniffle, then looked down and saw what was the matter.

"Shonda?"

"Daddy—"

"Where, uh, honey . . . where is your mother?" He couldn't remember where Sugar had gone.

"She went to run some errands, I think." Shonda didn't move from her spot in front of the sink. "Daddy, I think I better go to the hospital. Can you take me?"

Millard sprang into action. "Of course I can. Come here. Sit down and I'll go get your bag. You have a bag packed, don't you, Shonda? And what about shoes? Shonda, honey, where are your shoes?"

Millard got so worked up and they left the house in such a hurry that neither he nor Shonda thought to leave Sugar a note.

By the time Sugar figured out where they were, it was all over. Shonda had a quick labor and a dramatic delivery. Millard, so squeamish that he rarely flossed his teeth, had stayed with Shonda the whole time. When Sugar walked into the birthing room, Shonda was dozing and Millard was standing by the window, holding his new granddaughter.

He could not take his eyes off the baby, nor could he stop exclaiming over her. "Sugar, look at her! Isn't she beautiful?"

She was.

"Look at her eyes. They're so big! And those lashes!"

They were soft, long, and gently curled.

"Such perfect skin."

Like coffee with cream.

"See her hands and feet—ten perfect little fingers and toes."

Like dimpled, curled starfish they were.

"When can we bring her home?"

• • •

There is no way folks can keep from falling in love with Shonda's child, Millie Tonette Fry. The whole town of Ella Louise loves and claims her, as it does all its children. Yet folks agree there is something special about Shonda's girl. Little Millie is so pretty that strangers stop and ask to take her picture. She is so smart that last year she skipped third grade and went on to the fourth.

As for Millard—there are no words except to say that he is not the same. From the very moment he laid eyes on his granddaughter, Millard knew that he would and could fight a bear with his own two hands for the sake of little Millie.

At the hand of a child, Millard Fry became a changed man.

8

Blind Man's Bluff

Baby doctor Ed R. Meese, in all his years of taking care of children, did not recall seeing two babies who looked as much alike as did his new patients, six-month-old twins Polly Ann and Molly Jan Pierce. During their first visit to his office, while he examined Polly Ann, Dr. Meese inquired of their young mother, Sally Pierce. "Even identical twins generally have something different about them. Surely one of them has some sort of birthmark or identifying coloration that distinguishes her from her sister."

"No, sir. None that I've found," said Mrs. Pierce.

"A freckle, perhaps?" He shone a light into the baby's left ear, then her right one. After that, he pried open her rose-petal mouth with a tongue depressor and looked down her throat.

"No, sir."

"Hmm. Have you checked them for a cowlick, a widow's peak, or a swirl in their hair?"

"Neither of them has any of those, doctor."

"How do you tell them apart?" he asked.

"It's not easy." Sally laughed a nervous laugh. "When they were first born, I kept a little pink ribbon tied around Polly Ann's wrist, but then she got to where she could almost pull it off."

"So what do you do now?"

"See the bottoms of their shoes?" She turned one up so that he could see. "I took India ink and marked 'p's' on Polly Ann's and 'm's' on Molly Jan's."

"They don't pull their shoes off?"

"I tie the laces in double knots."

He nodded approval. "You're a clever mother to have kept these two little gals straight. No doubt as they get older, they'll develop some differences, and you'll learn which girl is which. Of course, by the time they're three or four they'll know their own names. But for now, I'd have to say that these two are as much a matched set as I've ever seen." He set Polly Ann to the side and reached for her twin. "You've got a healthy little girl here. Now let's take a look at Miss Molly Jan. Or are you Polly Ann?" He looked at his record. Scratching his head, he was suddenly confused.

"That's Molly," said Sally.

At home, Sally Pierce's shoe-marking system effectively kept her babies straight. She was careful to undress only one twin at a time, and she knew which baby slept in which bed. First thing every morning, she diapered and dressed one girl at a time. Before she put their shoes on, she checked the bottoms to make sure that the ink was clear. If the ink looked the least bit worn, she marked it again and blew on it until the ink dried.

The system worked well until one Sunday morning shortly after the twins learned to walk. In preparation for Sunday school and church, Sally bathed and dressed the girls in pink ruffled dresses, matching bonnets, socks, and their ink-marked shoes. Leaving the two of them standing by the back door ("Don't you two look pretty! Wait right here, and Mama will be right back."), she went back to her bedroom to get her Bible, where she took the time to stop and put another pin in her hair, change into a different pair of gloves, and wipe a smear of lipstick from her front teeth.

Taking full advantage of their mother's two-minute absence, Polly Ann and Molly Jan toddled to the bathroom and climbed, fully clothed, into the tub that their mother had neglected to drain.

That's where Sally, her Bible in hand and her hat on her head, found them. "Girls! Oh my goodness! What are you doing in the tub? Look at you. You're all wet!"

And they were. Soaked from the waist down. Dresses, petticoats, diapers, socks, and shoes—all of them wet.

SHOES?

No. Surely not. Please, God, no!

Sally plucked one girl from the tub, grasped her little ankle, and turned her foot over to see the sole of her shoe. Nothing but a smeared mess. She willed herself to stay calm. Maybe the other girl's shoe would be readable. Perhaps she hadn't been in the water as long as her sister. Maybe the ink on her shoe had set better. Sally set the first twin down and lifted the other out of the water. But her shoes too were marked only with a black blur of ink.

Mrs. Pierce sat down on the floor with a wet girl on each knee.

"Polly?"

"Molly?"

The girls gurgled and cooed. What now? Which girl was which? She had no idea.

And the honest truth? Neither do eighty-two-year-old housemates Molly and Polly. Oh, they thought they did. They'd never given their identity a bit of thought until twelve years ago, two months before their spry-till-the-end mother died at the age of ninety-six. On that day, their mother confessed to the unfortunate fact that the girls could have lived their entire lives mixed up.

"You mean I might be Molly?" Polly said.

"And I might be Polly?" Molly said.

"Girls, what was I to do? I was all alone with you two—your daddy was overseas in the service. There was no one to ask. You looked as alike then as you do now, and you sure didn't know your own names. After studying about it for a while, all I knew to do was to re-mark your shoes and put a pair on each of you."

"How did you decide which shoe to put on which one of us?" asked Polly.

"I sat you down, one on one corner of the sofa and one on the other. Then I got out the broom and drew two straws. I decided ahead of time that the first straw would be for the one on the left and the second for the one on the right. Whoever got the longest straw would be Polly, since she was born first. Whoever got the shorter straw would be Molly."

Molly didn't say anything, but she couldn't help but feel a bit cheated, getting the short straw and all.

"I felt real bad about it." The twins' mother twisted a tissue between her hands. "I reckon I should've told you the truth before now, but what kind of a mother doesn't know her own children? I never told anyone, not even your daddy, God rest his soul. I was too embarrassed."

The thought of the mix-up made Molly and Polly each a little dizzy, but not wanting to hurt their mother's feelings, they didn't let on.

"It's all right, Mother, we're still the same people as we were before," said Polly, patting her mama's hand.

"Nothing's changed," said Molly.

"May as well go on as before."

And so they did, living together in a pink house with faded lime-green shutters and a sea-blue-painted front porch. In their fenced yard they kept half a dozen peacocks that raised their heads and screamed, sounding just like panicked women, every time someone had the audacity to walk in their yard. "Watch birds" was how Molly described their feathered pets. "Better than a dog any day. Don't dig up the flower beds or tear up the newspaper." Every morning she sat on the porch and fed them peanuts from her flattened palm.

The Pierce sisters have lived together in Ella Louise for their whole lives and are a common sight around town. Both of them are slim and trim as a result of their daily walks to the post office, the Wild Flour, the grocery store, and the bank. Visitors who don't know Molly and Polly tend to be startled when they first cross paths with the red-haired pair. The sight of the sisters, zipped into identical, brightly colored wind suits, shielded from the sun by matching umbrellas held at the same jaunty angle, chewing their favorite Big Red gum in near-perfect synchronization, causes folks' jaws to drop. Long-time citizens, of course, don't give the girls a second thought.

"Good morning, ladies. Nice weather we're having, don't you think?" Mayor Tinker greeted them last week.

"Hello, Mayor. No, no problem with our sink," answered Molly. To her sister in what she intended to be a whisper, Molly said, "Town must not be paying him enough. Gone to doing plumbing on the side."

"You ladies need a lift?" asked Rochelle's husband after the pair had finished their once-a-week lunch at the Wild Flour. "Awful hot out there, and I'm going your way."

"Thank you, son, but we really don't need any hay," said Polly. "Could you come by later and change a couple of lightbulbs for us though?"

"Yes, ma'am. Got to pick up the children after school, but I can come by about three."

"Free? Of course you'd do it for free. That's what neighbors are for," Molly said as she winked.

The sisters, deaf as crackers, are entirely too vain to wear hearing aids. When their physician, Sarah Strickland, suggested they each get a set, they refused on the grounds of good health.

"I heard of a woman who wore them for just a week before she went so crazy that they had to put her away," Polly said. "Traced it all back to her hearing aid. She was normal as can be before she put it in."

"Cancer. They give you cancer. I read that somewhere. *Good Housekeeping*, I think it was," said Molly. "If God intended for folks to have mechanical instruments in their ears, he would have put them there. No siree. I will not be getting a hearing aid anytime soon. 'Sides, Sister and I can hear each other just fine."

"No, I don't have any dimes," said Polly. "Will two nickels do?"

With the exception of tasks like changing lightbulbs (neither of them had knees inclined to climb) and repairing the places in the fence where the peacocks could almost get out, Molly and Polly got along pretty well on their own. Their neighbors assured them of their willingness to help out, but Molly and Polly liked to do things for themselves.

Late on a recent Saturday evening, though, Molly and Polly admitted that help would have to be called.

Seems that Molly, who is plagued with dry skin, had accidentally poured in too much bath oil when she was taking her bath. After a long soak, she tried to get herself out of the tub but slipped and fell backwards. She wasn't hurt, but every time she tried to get up, she slipped back down. After thirty minutes of trying, she was so worn out that she could hardly move.

"Polly!" she called. "Polly, come here and help me!"

In about ten minutes, Polly finally heard her. "Oh my goodness! What happened? Are you all right? Did you go and break a hip? I hope not, because I am not about to go visit you in some home."

"Shush now. My hip's not broke. Come and help me get out of this tub."

Polly tried. With all her eighty-two years of might, she tried. She pulled. She pushed. She braced her feet and let Molly pull on her. All to no avail. No matter what they tried, Molly still could not get out. She would be almost, almost out, but she repeatedly slid back down.

Polly sat down on the toilet, exhausted but set on reasoning through the problem. "Sister, we've got to figure out what we're going to do."

Molly leaned back in the tub and covered her face with a towel. "I guess I could just live in the tub."

"I don't know as we have a choice but to call someone to come get you out," Polly finally replied.

"Don't you even think about it!" said Molly. "I am not going to have anyone come and see me like this. Besides, who would we call?"

"911."

"No! I won't have it."

"Mayor Tinker?"

"Sister, are you crazy? I'm naked!"

"What's your solution then?"

Molly studied for a minute, then said, "Call Tim."

"Tim? Tim who?"

"You know, that new fellow who's staying with the little girl who runs the Wild Flour. Her cousin, I think. Nice boy."

"The one from New Jersey? Sister, what are you thinking, having me call on a stranger for something like this?"

"Have you met him?"

"No. But I did see him come in and have lunch down at the Wild Flour. I didn't have occasion to speak to him."

"I saw him that day too, and while you were in the restroom, I met him. Rochelle made me acquainted with him. She said to me, 'Molly, I'd like you to meet my cousin Tim. He's from New Jersey. He's blind.' "

"Blind! Bless his heart." Polly was touched by the man's plight. "He sure gets around good, doesn't he?"

"Well, sure. They've got all kinds of schools and such for people like that up in New Jersey."

"I suppose so. As I recall, he didn't even have one of those white canes or a dog with him. Do you know how he lost his sight?"

"Got hit by a car or something. That doesn't matter. I want you to go in there, dial up the Wild Flour, and get the number where he's staying. Since he won't be able to see whether I've got on any clothes or not, he's who we'll get to help me out of this tub."

"You reckon he'll just come over here like that?"

Well, he did.

A strong, handsome man of twenty-seven, Tim

had Molly out of the tub on his first try. Didn't even have to strain.

"You don't know how much we appreciate this."

"No problem," Tim said. "I used to be a paramedic. Did this kind of thing all the time. Happens more than you think, you know. You ladies really ought to put a rubber mat down in your tub. Next time one of you could break a hip."

"That's what we've decided to do," Polly gushed. "Get us a mat for our tub. Won't you stay and have a piece of cake—German chocolate?"

"Sounds good."

"Coffee? It's decaf."

"I'd love some."

"So," Polly said, taking Tim's arm and guiding him to a kitchen chair. "I guess you can't do that kind of work anymore since you . . . since you . . . well, you know."

"I suppose I could, but I just got burned out on it. That happens to a lot of paramedics. The hours are long. The pay is good, but let me tell you, you earn every penny. After a few years, the stress got to be too much for me. That's when I went to drama school to be a mime. Not much call for that here in Ella Louise, but if I decide to stay, I might start holding classes for it down at the Chamber of Commerce."

Molly, dressed by then, was confused. "Classes? For the blind?"

"No, ma'am. For mime." He spoke up so she could hear. "*Mime.* You know. Acting?"

"You mean you're not . . ." Molly turned pale.

"Not what?"

"Oh, sister. He's not blind."

"Blind? No, ma'am. I've got twenty-twenty vision. I don't even have to wear contact lenses." He took a big gulp of coffee. "I don't mean to be greedy, but can I have another piece of cake?"

On Monday morning, Esther down at Dr. Strickland's office got the call. "Yes, ma'am. Yes, ma'am. I understand. Today? Well, I don't know. You'll need to call and see if they have any openings today. Emergency? Well, hold on a second, and I'll get you the number. Here it is. Have you got a pen? All right. The place that you're calling is the Clear Sound Hearing Aid Company. Dr. Strickland recommends them to all her patients. Says that they do good work and sell a fine product . . . Hello?"

The woman had already hung up.

"Guess the Pierce sisters finally decided to give it up and get hearing aids. About time."

Past time, Polly and Molly would say. Past time indeed.

9

Pinkie and the Chief

Upon meeting Chief Johnson for the first time, most expect that he, the owner and curator of Ella Louise's American Indian Arrowhead and Artifact Museum, will have a liberal lean. Nothing could be further from the truth, and such assumptions pain Chief.

"For crying out loud," a visitor recently observed, "the guy was wearing a silver and turquoise watchband. He has a teepee in his front yard. Gotta be just a little bit weird, if you ask me." The visitor's disrespectful comments were overheard by Ella Louise's mayor, Alfred Tinker, and his secretary, Faye Beth Newman. Generally an even-tempered pair, the two of them did not take kindly to the insult directed toward one of the town's good citizens. By the time they got through speaking their minds to the out-of-towner, he had been corrected on things he wasn't even aware of being mistaken about. So repentant was he of his careless words that on his way out of town, he stopped and made a donation to Chief's fine museum.

But truthfully, Chief *is* an unusual fellow, and it's no great stretch to understand why those who don't know any better take a fellow like Chief to be the same kind of person who would worship the sun, dance naked for rain, or beat on a drum.

Even vote Democrat.

If given the chance, Chief can explain about the teepee and the watchband. He spent years researching, gathering materials, and preparing to construct his teepee. It was a twenty-year dream of his to create one that would be historically accurate. (You wouldn't know it, but those things are bigger than what they look like on TV.) Chief was well into the building of the structure when he realized that the only place it would fit was right in front of his house. And as for his eye-catching watchband? It was a gift from his sweet little mother, God rest her soul. She bought the piece at an Indian gift shop while on a bus trip to Carlsbad, New Mexico, unaware that it was too gaudy for a man. Since the watchband was the last gift she gave Chief before passing away, he wears it every day.

So no, Chief Johnson is not a worshipper of the sun. He's an upright and moral man; he's been a deacon in the Baptist church for the past decade and is a member in good standing of the Ella Louise Elect More Republicans Club.

Of course, some folks still have trouble understanding why a normal man would even want a teepee in his front yard. Chief's fascination with Indian stuff goes back to his Aunt Effie, who first got him interested in it. Starting the year he turned ten (at that time he was still called by his given name, Bill) and continuing through his lanky-legged teenage years, Chief would spend ten days every summer with his aunt. Aunt Effie didn't have any kids of her own. She didn't even have a husband—but she wore blue jeans, and she sure was fun.

During his summertime visits, Bill and his aunt never did just stay at home. Year after year, the two of them hit the road, camping out together.

Bill always arrived on the Friday 3:00 P.M. bus, and Aunt Effie was always there at the station to pick him up. They talked all the way to her house and stayed up half the night studying the map, going over their route. Early the next morning, they headed out in her car packed with sleeping bags and a tent, a bunch of mustard and bologna sandwiches, iodine tablets, and half a dozen quart jars of home-canned peaches. For one week every year, they traveled all over Colorado and New Mexico. They hiked, panned for real gold, visited Indian tourist sites, ate fry bread, and explored the ruins of old villages.

It was on the first of their trips that Bill found his first arrowhead. Though less than an inch long and sporting a broken tip, it was a real arrowhead all the same. Bill was so proud of his find that he couldn't stop pulling it out of his pocket to look at it. Wow! Made by an actual Indian. Someone who lived a really long time ago.

When they got back to her house, Aunt Effie fixed him up a cardboard cigar box lined with a red velvet cloth so he could display it in his room when he got home.

Every year after that one, Bill found more arrowheads. He also collected bits of pottery. So good was he at finding such things that in five years' time, three bookshelves in his room had been given over to a growing collection of Indian artifacts.

As Bill got older, his interest in Indians didn't wane. He read books about Indians, visited museums about Indians, and took the bus to Houston to see traveling exhibits about Indians. Bill even traced his family tree back three generations and discovered that two of his ancestors actually had some Indian blood in them, which meant that he had some too. Navajo, as best as he could determine.

So great was his passion for all things Indian that by the time he was sixteen, Bill's friends and most of his family began calling him "Chief." It started out as a joke, but the name fit so well that it stuck, and now most folks don't even know that he used to be Bill.

Today, Chief's collection of artifacts are housed

in a climate-controlled portable building that sits to the east of his house. Inside, he has done a great job organizing and creating interesting displays. With his own hands he built lighted, floor-to-ceiling shelves that hold all kinds of cool Indian stuff. Along with arrowheads and pottery, Chief displays Indian jewelry and clothing, Indian blankets and carvings, and Indian tools. One corner of the museum houses a library of books, which Chief is glad to lend out as long as people sign for them. He also has a little TV and VCR set up and a collection of educational videos that do a good job explaining Indian culture and lore.

Folks from all over have visited Chief's museum. He doesn't charge any admission, but he does keep a guest book. In the dozen years that he's had the place open, Chief has hosted visitors from eight different states, as well as families from Mexico and Canada.

People from Ella Louise love to visit the museum too. Along with boring stuff like multiplication tables and state capitals, a trip to the Indian museum is on the agenda of every fifth-grade class that passes through Ella Louise Elementary. The kids love to come; they look forward to it all year. After Chief's given them the tour and showed them his best video, he builds a fire and cooks fry bread, which they eat together, sitting Indian style inside the teepee.

• • •

It was in part because of the good times he enjoyed with his Aunt Effie that Chief even considered taking into his house his New York City sister Chesley's fourteen-year-old grandson, Pinkie.

Chesley had always been a fast talker. This time, as usual, she ran on and on. Pinkie's single-parent mother, Chesley's daughter, had been called upon to spend the entire summer working overseas. No one in the young man's immediate family, including her, was available to keep him. His mother was at her wit's end. And she had come up with the great idea to see if perhaps Chief would look after Pinkie. It would only be for two months. He was a good boy, Pinkie was —typical teenager, you know how they are— and would be no trouble.

"Chesley, I'm flattered that you thought of me, but why send the boy here? I haven't seen him since he was about three. There's not much for a kid to do in Ella Louise. Well, yes. Yes. I understand. How about you give me till tomorrow to think it over? I promise. I will. All right. Goodbye."

Chief did think it over. He sat up most of the night thinking it over. By morning, he had not come up with a single good reason to say no. Actually, he told himself, this shouldn't be so hard. He had been a fourteen-year-old boy once.

He remembered what it was like. Things couldn't have changed much.

Finally, Chief gave it up. He decided that he would do his best to show the boy a good time. A really good time. Shoot, he would take the boy exploring and camping, maybe to the dry river bottom where folks still found Indian artifacts with surprising regularity. Maybe they'd even join the Boy Scouts—surely the Boy Scouts had some kind of summer program. Come to think about it, the kid might already be a Boy Scout. Wouldn't that be fun! And didn't the Boy Scouts have some kind of badge or patch you could get for learning about Indian lore? Chief bet that such a badge would be hard to get living in New York City. Why, Pinkie would have it made in the shade. He'd be the envy of all of his friends. Imagine the paper Pinkie would write on what he did during his summer vacation. He, Chief, would personally see to it that Pinkie had a lot to say.

In preparation for the young scout's arrival, Chief bought new sheets for the sofa bed and stocked up on groceries, laying in a big supply of beef jerky, which made a great snack and would be easy to pack when they went camping.

"Which flight are you putting him on? All right. That will be fine. I'll be there at the airport to meet him. You're welcome. No, he won't be any trouble. You don't worry about a thing. We'll be just fine."

Pinkie missed his flight.

He must have, Chief reasoned, because there was no one in the group of passengers coming off Pinkie's flight that could be his nephew.

"Uncle Bill?"

Chief jumped at the voice behind him, then turned to face it and jumped again.

"Excuse me, but are you my Uncle Bill? Bill Johnson? Are you, uh, the *Chief?*" Pinkie looked a bit confused. I mean, the man didn't have a braid or anything (didn't Indians wear braids?), but he *was* wearing a green windbreaker, which was what Pinkie's grandmother had told him Uncle Bill would have on.

"Yes, I am. But you wouldn't be . . . I mean, you're not . . . ." Chief's voice trailed off hopefully.

"Yeah, I'm Pinkie."

Chief didn't know whether to hug the nephew he hadn't seen in twelve years or put him back on the plane.

Likewise, six-foot-two-inch Pinkie, sporting spiked hair, three earrings, and sagging, ragged, three-sizes-too-big jeans, looked like he didn't know whether he should shake the hand of his uncle or get back on the plane.

Oh my. Earrings? Chesley hadn't mentioned them. What did it mean to have three in one ear?

Chief racked his brain. He thought he remembered that *one* earring used to mean *something,* but if a person has *three,* does that cancel out the meaning of *one?*

Chief was sure the Boy Scouts didn't allow such things.

"Son," Chief whispered so as not to embarrass the young man, "your underpants are showing."

Pinkie looked confused, like he hadn't heard him, so Chief, as unobtrusively as he could, motioned in the general direction of Pinkie's rear—a skinny rear, clad in royal blue boxers with tan monkey faces on them that were visible a good six or eight inches above his pants.

"Oh, uh, thanks." Pinkie gave his jeans a tug. "Should we go and get my bag, you think?"

Pinkie and Chief stood side by side, separated in height by a good six inches if you counted Pinkie's hair. Neither of them spoke but instead concentrated on locating Pinkie's bag on the luggage carousel. When Pinkie spotted the bag and pointed it out, Chief moved forward to retrieve it. Funny, Uncle Bill didn't look like any Indian Pinkie had ever seen in movies. The guy had *red* hair, was wearing polyester pants, and was not wearing moccasins but instead silver sneakers with Velcro! Hadn't his grandma said that he was going to stay with an Indian chief?

No way. The man drove a twelve-year-old Buick. Four door.

Their silence continued till they got out on the road. Finally, on the highway headed toward Ella Louise, Chief said to Pinkie, "We've got at least three hours ahead of us. 'Bout supper time. Are you hungry?"

Pinkie, seeing the Golden Arches up ahead, could not contain his grin. Uncle Bill had read his mind. "I sure am. They gave us stuff to eat on the plane, but it wasn't very good." He could already taste a Big Mac, french fries, and a Coke.

"I knew I remembered right. Boys your age, well, you can't fill 'em up. Uh, Pinkie, reach down there under the seat, back between your feet."

Pinkie bent to look.

"Find a paper sack? Yeah, that's it. And a thermos? You may have to reach back pretty far for it. May have rolled. I packed some sandwiches—tuna, with lots of pickles and boiled egg—and a quart of cold sweet milk. That ought to hit the spot."

Tuna? Pinkie unwrapped a sandwich. Stuff sort of stunk. People eat this? His mother never cooked. Not even tuna. Pinkie was accustomed to food that came wrapped in some kind of plastic wrapper, Styrofoam package, or cardboard box.

"Go on. Those are all for you. I ate before I started out," said Chief.

Pinkie took a bite and tried not to gag. He wrapped the sandwich back up. "You know, I'm pretty tired, and I'm sort of a vegetarian. Maybe I'll wait and eat something later."

Pinkie dug headphones out of his bag, put them on, leaned against the door, and pretended sleep.

On the ride home, Chief snuck long glances at Pinkie's strange hair, his piercings, and his choice of clothing. He came to the realization that Pinkie was not of the sort to join the Boy Scouts. Nor did he look to be the kind of boy interested in exploring the river or going camping or hiking. A kid from New York? A city kid? Spending time outdoors? What had he been thinking? It had been a foolish notion, Chief determined, to expect to spend the summer showing the kid around.

Chief steered the car off the freeway and let his thoughts ramble. No fool like an old fool. A boy like Pinkie was not going to be interested in Indian stuff, camping out, or hikes in the woods. He probably wished he was back in New York, going to rock concerts or whatever it was city kids did these days. And who could blame him? Wasn't like it was Pinkie's fault.

Chief made the decision then and there to cut young Pinkie some slack. He'd set a few rules, give the boy a wide berth, and go on about things like Pinkie wasn't there. It had been a mistake for the boy to come, but two months wasn't all that long.

"No drugs, no drinking, no loud music, and we'll get along fine," is how Chief explained things over lunch the next day. "There's a TV in the living room. You can watch all you want. Fix whatever you want to eat—there's peanut butter and cheese. Just clean up after yourself. Understand?"

Pinkie did.

"All right, then. I'll be back after a while." It was Tuesday, museum day. Chief grabbed the keys off the hook by the door.

Pinkie sat at the table and stared at the door. Not a word about the teepee or the museum, both of which he was dying to see. Had he done something wrong? He didn't know what. But it didn't matter. He'd gotten the message loud and clear that Chief wished he wasn't here. Fine. He could take a hint.

And so for the first two weeks, though he hated being inside, that's where Pinkie stayed—parked in front of the television or sprawled on the sofa bed, listening to music. Few people in Ella Louise even realized that Chief had company— which, honestly, considering how Pinkie looked, didn't bother Chief all that much.

Yet Chief reported to Chesley when she called, "Everything's going fine."

"It's okay, Grandma," said Pinkie when it was his turn to talk.

But it wasn't. It was lonely and awkward and not what either of them had had in mind. The only good thing? Just six more weeks to go. And so far, they really hadn't had any problems.

Until Chief found cigarette ashes in the teepee. He didn't have reason to enter the teepee often these days, but on a Sunday evening when he went inside the structure to retrieve a pottery bowl he planned to use for a special display in the museum, Chief discovered a nasty pile of ashes, butts, and black-tipped matches. He sat himself down and gazed at the evidence staring him in the face. He was shocked—and hurt. What was Pinkie thinking, sneaking out here to smoke? Chief had thought things were going okay, considering. They'd had no words, no arguments, no conflict of any kind. How could Pinkie have done such a thing? How could he have been so foolish as to leave the evidence for anyone to find it?

What should he do? Confront the boy? Ignore what he knew? Punish him?

Chief decided it was best to catch the boy in the act—which turned out to be no easy task. Several mornings in a row, Chief found fresh evidence that Pinkie had been smoking inside the teepee, but after several tries, he still had not caught Pinkie at it.

"I'm going over to Pearly to pick up some

groceries. You know, they've got a wholesale place over there. I'll be gone at least three hours," Chief baited Pinkie before going down to the Wild Flour so as to kill an hour before sneaking back home. When he came back home, he parked the Buick around back and eased around the side of the house to get a peek inside the teepee.

No Pinkie.

"Whew! I'm tired," Chief said the next night. "I think I'll head on to bed early tonight. You know, I'm so tired I bet I'll sleep like a rock."

Chief set his alarm clock for midnight. But when, at the sound of the alarm, he crept out of bed, Pinkie was still in his—sound asleep and snoring. Yet the next morning? Fresh ashes in the teepee again.

Confound it! Outwitted by a fourteen-year-old kid. Just wasn't right.

Then Chief came up with a surefire plan. That night, once Pinkie was asleep, or at least pretending to sleep, Chief crept out of bed, put on his shoes, and slipped out the back door. He padded around to the front yard, unfastened the leather-laced flap of the teepee, and let himself in. When Pinkie snuck in to smoke, he would be waiting.

Chief got a bit sleepy, waiting in the tent, and dozed off. When he woke up an hour later, he was disoriented and startled from a dream in which he was falling. It took a few seconds for him to get his bearings, but when he did, he heard foot-steps on the other side of the teepee.

The flap lifted and a sneaker-clad foot stepped inside.

Chief sat frozen in his spot.

Another sneaker-clad foot. Then, surprisingly, four more. In the dark, the feet were all Chief could see. Six in all. Not only was Pinkie sneaking out here to smoke, he was meeting other teen hoodlums too! Chief heard whispers, but it was still too dark to see who the voices belonged to. He managed to stay still, to bide his time, but it wasn't easy!

Finally, matches were lit, and after several attempts, so were cigarettes. Three of them. Then coughs, low voices, and nervous laughter.

Enough. Trembling with anger, Chief stood up, turned on his flashlight, and shined it into the faces of Pinkie and his cohorts. Except it wasn't Pinkie at all. The smoking trio turned out to be Jessica Martin, Marcie Billingsly, and Alicia Turner—sputtering, terrified fifth graders who only last month had been treated to fry bread on this very spot.

When the light hit their eyes, the three girls froze; then they screamed, dropped their ciga-rettes and matches, and nearly brought the teepee down as they scrambled over each other in their hurry to get out.

"Wait! Stop!" Chief was so surprised to see the

little girls that he could barely get the words out.

"Uncle Bill? Are you in here?" It was Pinkie. Sleeping in the front room only a few feet from the teepee, Pinkie had been awakened by the commotion and now stood blinded by the flashlight Chief shone in his eyes. "Uncle Bill! What's going on? There's smoke in here!" Pinkie stepped inside and began stomping at a flaming rug onto which the girls had dropped their cigarettes.

"Gracious!" said Chief, so shocked that he stood rooted to the floor. Asthmatic, he was already coughing and wheezing from the smoke.

"Uncle Bill, get out of here." Pinkie shoved him toward the door. "Go on! Get out!"

Chief managed to stumble out the door, but not before inhaling enough smoke to cause him to fall to his knees, gasping for breath.

Pinkie stayed in the teepee long enough to stomp out the fire, then joined Chief outside. "Uncle Bill? Are you okay? Should I call 911?"

Chief, who couldn't speak, shook his head no.

So Pinkie helped him into a lawn chair instead.

"Lean back, Uncle Bill. Breath real slow." Without being asked, Pinkie ran inside the house and brought out Chief's inhaler.

"Thank you," Chief gasped. He took two puffs. Within a couple of minutes, he was still coughing, but his breathing had slowed. In ten minutes, he was all right.

"Son," Chief said after he'd settled down, "you

were something tonight—putting out the fire, helping me get out. Getting me this." He held up his inhaler. "That was quick thinking. Most kids—lands, Pinkie—most *adults* would have panicked. Where did you get such a cool head?"

Embarrassed, Pinkie looked away. "I dunno. Scouts, I guess."

"Boy Scouts?"

"Yeah. Been in 'em since I was a kid. They teach you a lot. You know. Fire safety. First aid. That kind of stuff."

Chief couldn't help himself. "They let you be in Scouts with your, your . . ."

Pinkie put his hand to his ear. "You mean these? Oh, I don't wear 'em. Scoutmaster says he knows they don't mean anything, but not everybody understands things that way. When I do stuff with Scouts, I take 'em out. It's no big deal."

Suddenly, painfully, Chief could see that it was not.

If you ever are in Ella Louise, don't miss stopping by Chief's museum. He's made a lot of improvements in the past several years. The teepee no longer stands alone in his front yard. Now the structure is the focal point of a painstakingly authentic Indian household scene, complete with appropriate transplanted native plants, tools, hunting implements, and a clay oven that really bakes. Seeing the teepee is an

146

interesting, educational experience, and one that I enjoy every time I visit.

You should know that Chief didn't do all this by himself. There's no way that he could have. When visitors marvel at the detail of the Indian scene, Chief is quick to explain that his nephew, Pinkie, an Eagle Scout, comes every summer, all the way from New York, to help him out.

Fine boy, that Pinkie is. Yes, sir. Fine boy— earrings and all.

10

Scared Crow

Crow Buxley liked to pick pecans. He enjoyed the whole process of cracking their shells, prying out the meat, and—lacking a pie-baking wife—eating them out of hand. Somewhat of an expert on the wiles of nature, Crow could predict by the shell thickness of this year's crop that Ella Louise was in for an unusually early fall and first frost.

Some folks scoffed at Crow's weather forecasting abilities. When they did, he pointed out that if this year's hardy pecan shells didn't appear convincing enough, the dense coats worn by his yard's nut-loving gang of squirrels should be proof enough for anyone.

So sure was Crow of his prediction that at the end of August, when Dinty Moore beef stew, tapioca pudding mix, and Martha White yellow cornmeal went on sale, he laid in a heavy supply of each. Crow knew that nothing hit the spot on a chilly day like stew and cornbread, topped off with tapioca pudding. He also timed the planting of his fall garden so as to complete his harvest early.

Unwilling to let anyone be caught unprepared, Crow did his best to convince his neighbors that they should do the same. But August turned out to be unusually hot, with temperatures staying in the one hundreds for more than a week in a row, and few folks heeded his warnings. By the first of September, things hadn't cooled down much, but Crow was undeterred; he began working at getting his garden ready for winter.

His neighbor down the road, Bessie Bishop, who had been widowed just about a year ago, detoured into his garden on her morning walk. "Harvesting your greens and your squash already?" she asked. "Hardly big enough to cook, are they?"

"Not aiming to lose 'em. In the cold. You know." Crow, kneeling between the rows, just hated the way he talked around Bessie. Lately, his voice tended to squeak, and on occasion he could hardly get his words out. "Gonna come an early frost. Hard one."

"Early frost? Crow!" She put her hand on her hip in a way that Crow thought was so cute. "Almanac says we're not likely to get a freeze until middle of November. You're squandering a good part of your growing season."

"You ought to be getting your vegetables picked too. Be a shame to lose what you've been working on all summer."

Crow suddenly realized that from his position

on his knees he could see a good three inches of Bessie's slip. White. Two rows of lace. Embarrassed, he looked down and said gruffly, "If you need any help, let me know."

Crow's prediction turned out to be correct. By the tenth of October the air had taken on a chilly feel, which was early for a Southern climate such as Ella Louise. Then began almost a full week of cold, drizzly rain.

And then came Crow's predicted hard freeze. Overnight, the temperature dropped so quickly that his neighbors woke up to the sounds of their cats howling to come in and to the sight of yesterday's green gardens turned shriveled, dark, and slimy.

"Told you." Crow couldn't resist niggling Bessie as he helped her salvage what little she could of her tomatoes. "Signs were everywhere. Plain as the scab on a first-grader's knee."

"If you'll quit that gloating, I might be talked into frying us up some of these underripes."

"That sounds pretty good." Crow feigned nonchalance. "Hand them 'maters over and I'll wash them off under the outside hydrant so as to keep your kitchen sink clean."

"Nice of you."

Over their shared supper, Bessie and Crow discussed what plans they had for the upcoming week.

"Granddaughter's coming Wednesday," said Crow.

"One that's expecting a baby?" asked Bessie.

"Uh-huh. Angie. And she already knows that the baby's gonna be a little boy."

"How nice for her. Don't they already have two girls?"

"Yep. With those two, we didn't know what we were getting, but this time Angie went and had herself analyzed."

Suddenly Crow was overcome with embarrassment. He looked at his plate and tried to figure out how to undo what he had just done. What had come over him, to bring up female matters in mixed company? He knew better. He'd certainly been raised better. Hearing Angie speak about things so matter-of-fact caused him to let down his guard. Young folks these days didn't think nothing about talking about anything with anyone.

"Bessie, I didn't mean . . ."

"Was it an ultrasound or an amnio?" she asked.

"Pardon me?"

"Well, if it was an ultrasound, sometimes those are wrong. But an amnio, well, that test is almost a sure thing."

Crow didn't know which test it was, but he did know that he was ready to talk about something else. "Bessie, could I trouble you for a toothpick?"

Bessie got up to get him one from where she kept them on the windowsill above the sink. Staring out the window, she observed, "Gonna be lots of leaves this year. They're already starting to fall. I tell you, raking leaves is one job I could do without. Makes my hay fever act up. And all that bending and stooping—my lower back aches just thinking about it. I dread doing it every year."

"Really? I don't mind raking so much." Crow sat up straighter in his chair. He could be her knight in shining armor—or at least her yard man. "Soon as I get mine all done up, I'll come take care of yours. I imagine I can have 'em raked and bagged in a morning, and you can make me some lunch. Deal?"

That sounded like a deal to Bessie.

By the next Saturday, Crow had raked, piled, and bagged his own yard, front and back. It was amazing how much tidier a place could look with only a day's worth of cleaning up. He still needed to dig up his beds, but that could wait until he got Bessie's leaves raked.

"Coffee before you get started?" Bessie asked from her porch. She was looking pretty as a picture.

"Naw. I already had a whole pot. If I drink any more I'll have to . . ." *There I go again!* Crow grimaced and wiped at his mouth. *What is wrong with me? Why, if my daddy was alive, he'd kill me dead for discussing such things around a woman . . .* "I'm fine. You go on inside. Let me get to work."

"Suit yourself."

Crow raked all morning. Even in the chilly air, he worked up a sweat. By noon, the sun had come out, and he shed his jacket. "Bessie," Crow asked after he'd finished the good lunch that she'd delivered, "I got off without a hankie this morning, and I need something to wipe my brow with. Sweat's stinging my eyes. Have you got some old rag or a bandana I could use?"

The pink washrag she got him worked just fine. He folded it up and tucked it into the loose-fitting waistband of his pants. The rag came in handy, and he used it several times.

Bessie had more leaves in her yard than Crow had first thought. By 3:00 his back was complaining, and he took her up on the offer of a cold cola on the back patio. They sat in lawn chairs and looked at what he'd gotten done so far. "Almost finished," he reported after a long swig. "All that's really left is that big gully up next to the fence."

"Wind's blown a bunch of 'em up in there. It's pretty deep," observed Bessie. "You best be careful. Could be snakes in that ditch. Copperheads'd be my guess. You know, I saw on the nature channel that copperheads like nothing better than to curl up under damp leaves so as to go to sleep for the winter. I don't reckon it would be a good thing to wake up some cranky ole reptile. You wearing gloves?"

"Yes, ma'am."

"Well." Bessie rose to her feet. "I'll be getting back to my ironing."

"I'll get back to those leaves."

"You don't know how much I appreciate you doing this for me, Crow."

"Show me." Emboldened by fatigue, he asked, "Bessie, will you go with me tonight to eat at the café? This is Friday, isn't it? Rochelle'll be serving catfish. All you can eat." His heart palpitating at what he'd gone and done, Crow held his breath. This was new territory. He and Bessie had never been out on a . . . on a date. Would she go?

Bessie stood looking up at the sky for a moment, then said, "Okay."

"Okay, then."

Crow got so excited at the thought of enjoying Bessie's company over coleslaw and hush puppies that he went back to his raking with renewed vigor. Inspired perhaps, too, by the thought of dining on seafood, he, who couldn't sing a lick, caught himself humming the theme from *Love Boat*.

It was not until Crow got deeper into the pile of leaves that his vigorous raking and shoving of leaves into plastic bags slowed. Mixed in with the leaves were a lot of twigs and branches, long-dead weeds, and twisted vines. Seeing those vines, Crow couldn't help but dwell on what Bessie had said about snakes. He hated snakes. His cousin got bit by one once. The snap of a twig made Crow jump. He hoped Bessie wasn't watching through the window.

Crow took to cautiously turning the leaves over a time or two with his rake before reaching down with his hands to scoop them into the bag. Even though he had gloves on, Crow reasoned that a snake could probably bite right through.

An hour of turning and churning the dead vegetation resulted in only a few spooked spiders, some sleepy-eyed lizards, and a startled pair of brown toads.

No snakes. At least that he saw.

Well, Crow never did see one. No, he felt it. Inside his right pant leg. Soft, kind of loopy, just below his knee, but not moving at all. Crow stood stock-still.

It moved.

Crow froze.

It eased down to his ankle.

Crow's heart pounded. Sweat broke out on his head. He tried to scream, but nothing came out.

Finally, Crow threw his rake down and charged in the direction of Bessie's front door. Every few steps, he'd pause, shake his leg, and wildly try to get shed of his pants. Not until he was right in front of Bessie's picture window did Crow manage to get a hold of himself long enough to kick off his shoes and pull off his pants.

Bessie, a retired nurse, had seen just about everything on a man that there was to see. But when she stepped out into the yard to shake out a rug, she drew in a startled breath when she saw Crow, in his green undershorts, poking at his pants with a stick.

"Crow?"

He motioned for her to stand clear. "Snake," he panted, his eyes not moving from the bulge in his dungarees that now lay on the ground. "In my pant leg."

"Oh my goodness!"

"Bessie, have you got a hoe?"

"Of course. I'll go get it. Are you all right? Did you get bitten? Should I call 911?"

"Nah. Just get me the hoe."

Once Bessie handed him the hoe, he proceeded to chop his pants to smithereens. Only after a good dozen hacks did he think it safe to have a look.

"Stay back," he cautioned Bessie. "He may not be dead yet."

Bessie covered her eyes. "Tell me when it's safe to look."

Crow hooked the end of Bessie's hoe through a belt loop in his shredded pants, raised the pants high, and gave them a gentle shake.

"Is it dead?" Bessie asked from behind her cupped hands.

"Don't know. Still in there." Crow gave his pants another shake.

"What about now?"

"Uh . . ."

"What kind of a snake is it?"

"It's uh . . . not exactly . . . uh . . ."

Curiosity got the better of Bessie and she uncovered her eyes. Too far back to see the snake, she eased over toward the pants. Uncertain, she stayed behind Crow for protection, took hold of his arm, and leaned forward to take a look.

"Crow?"

She pushed up her glasses.

"Yes." He looked for someplace to duck.

"That's not a snake."

She had that right.

"That's my pink washrag. Chopped to pieces."

Who would have guessed that a sweat-soaked washrag sliding down from one's waistband would feel exactly like the creeping of a dangerous reptile? Suddenly, like Adam in the garden, Crow became acutely aware of his pantsless state.

"Crow?" Bessie said, politely averting her eyes. "Want me to drive you home so you can put on some pants?"

Crow nodded his head and tried to hide himself behind the rake.

"By the way, the yard looks real nice."

"Thanks," he said, staring at the ground.

"Crow?"

He looked up just in time to catch her wink.

"My mama raised a conservative girl. Though those are some attractive green undershorts you've got on, if it's all the same to you, do you think you could keep your pants on when I'm around?"

Crow told no one about what had happened to him over at Bessie's house. No one, that is, save his granddaughter, Angie.

"Aw, Gramps," said Angie. "I wouldn't worry about it. Besides, it really could have been a snake. You could have been bitten. And if it had turned out to be a poisonous snake, why, you could have died or at least gotten really sick." She pushed her hair out of her eyes. "Come on, Gramps," she said. "There's a bright side to everything."

Yeah, there was. That was the point. There was a bright side, all right, and Bessie Bishop had gotten a good look at it!

11

Wise Woman

Every single Tuesday, Faye Beth Newman receives a bouquet of flowers from her husband, Harvey. Sometimes she gets daisies, other times it's red roses or pink carnations. As soon as the florist delivers the new batch, Faye Beth tosses last week's flowers in the garbage. She displays the fragrant arrangements on the corner of her desk at the Chamber of Commerce, where she has worked for the past seven years. Though Faye Beth throws the old flowers away, she saves the vases. Harvey doesn't know it, but to help him out, every month or so she gathers the vases up and takes them down to the florist so that they can be used again. Harvey gets a discount because of it.

Since the Chamber of Commerce shares a building with Tawny's Quick Tan, a lot of folks come in and out of the building. Faye Beth's flowers always draw attention.

Last Tuesday an arrangement of lemon-yellow daylilies graced her desk. The flowers caught the eye of Janet Evans, who had stopped in to

159

fuss to the mayor about some potholes in front of her house. "You're still getting flowers every week? Harvey's so romantic. I'm lucky if my Ray remembers to send me a single rose on our anniversary. Last year he got me a weed whacker and a new pair of garden gloves. Now, does that make a gal's heart go a-flutter or what?"

"You get flowers every week? For how many years?" asked Rochelle Shartle, who had just come in to tan.

"Eleven."

"I'd say that man of yours is a keeper," said Rochelle.

"I didn't always think so."

"Come on! You and Harvey? Why, you two act like newlyweds! Harvey was bragging on you just the other day," said Janet. "He told Dr. Strickland that you get up at 4:30 in the morning just to fix his cereal."

"At 4:30?" said Rochelle. "Why?"

"Harvey works the early shift. He has to leave the house at 5:15," explained Faye Beth.

"And he can't pour his own bowl of Fruit Loops?"

"Harvey likes his cereal soft. I get up when he does so I can pour the milk on it for him while he's in the shower. That way it's ready to eat when he gets out," said Faye Beth, as if that explained everything.

Rochelle's jaw just about hit her chest.

"It's not so bad. Once I've got it fixed, I go back to bed."

"Girl! You have got that man spoiled!" exclaimed Janet.

"Some people are just made for each other," said Rochelle. "I suppose you and Harvey have never had a cross word."

Faye Beth snorted loudly and some of the diet Pepsi she was drinking came out of her nose. "Honey, have you ever driven by my house?"

"I don't think so," said Rochelle.

"You, Janet?"

"No, I haven't. Don't you and Harvey live way out down some little road past the cemetery?"

"We do. In a double-wide trailer. Harvey bought it before we were married. If you ever come out to see me, you're gonna see that we've got a pretty little place. Lots of trees and flowers. Our trailer's real nice too. The week before we were married, Harvey built a free-standing raised roof—set on steel poles—over the top of the trailer so as to make it safer for me. Harvey was proud as could be of that roof. He planned it, designed it, and set, framed, and shingled it himself. You know, a trailer isn't the safest place to live, but it was what Harvey and I could afford. He said that roof would offer protection should a storm or something come up."

"Good idea."

"Would be, except it's got a big piece of it all tore up."

"Big wind?"

"You could say that," Faye Beth laughed.

Single until she was thirty-nine years old, Faye Beth Newman, bride of Harvey, did not take to marriage right off. "Harvey, Harvey," he heard her hiss on their December wedding night. "Move over. I'm on the edge of the bed. And give me some cover. I'm freezing."

Accustomed to sleeping alone, Faye Beth had a terrible time adjusting to a divvied-up bed. She, an only child, had never shared a bedroom, much less a bed. And Harvey, plagued with seasonal sinus trouble—bless his heart—sniffed, snored, and snorted something terrible when he slept. He also tossed and turned so much that every morning the fitted sheets were torn from both corners on his side of the bed. It was six months into their union before Faye Beth got to where she could get some semblance of a good night's sleep.

A bed wasn't the only thing Faye Beth had trouble sharing. When she and Harvey shopped for groceries together, they each picked out what snacks they liked best. Though she didn't want to appear selfish, it rankled Faye Beth when she would reach into the refrigerator with her mouth all set for her favorite low-fat, cherry-vanilla yogurt, only to find that Harvey had eaten the last carton during one of his middle-of-the-night food forages.

"Harvey, honey, if you want cherry-vanilla yogurt, just tell me and I'll buy it for you," Faye Beth said in her sweetest voice.

"No need to do that, sugar. If I get a hankering, I'll just have some of yours."

Faye Beth took to hiding her yogurt in the vegetable bin of the refrigerator. Her snack was safe there, because Harvey's favorite vegetable was spaghetti.

Then there was the checkbook. Unwisely counseled that truly committed couples share a single bank account, she and Harvey opened one together, which worked out fine until their first bank statement arrived. Comparing it to Harvey's register in the back of his checkbook, Faye Beth got all confused.

"Harvey, darling, what do you mean you round all your checks up to the next highest dollar?"

"I'll show you. It works like this. When I write a check for say, $23.37, I write it down as $24.00. If it's for $19.79, I write $20.00. That way I know we always have more money in the bank than we think we do. Haven't bounced a check in twelve years. Pretty clever, huh?"

Marriage. What had sounded like a good idea to Faye Beth when she and Harvey were courting turned out to be not what she had expected at all. During the first few months of their union, she stuffed down a lot of what she felt inside. That didn't work for long. By their first anniversary, she had quit stuffing and had given herself over to irritability. Faye Beth still loved Harvey; she just didn't like him very much. Seemed that no matter what he did, it made her mad.

As for Harvey? He, who hated conflict, couldn't believe the sour turn his life had taken since he'd married Faye Beth. As a single man, he had been able to do things just the way he pleased. If he had known that marriage to Faye Beth was going to be like this, he would have given it some more thought.

To make matters worse, the couple differed in the ways that they dealt with their unhappiness. Faye Beth made a loud fuss over just about everything. Harvey feigned contentment.

"She's just a bit high strung, is all" was how he explained Faye Beth spinning their Chevy out of the church parking lot, leaving him to find his own ride home because she was tired and he, in her opinion, had stood around and talked way too long. *What? An hour was too long?*

"She's a good woman, just got a lot on her mind," Harvey offered as an excuse when at a yard sale she stomped her foot and threatened to leave him for good if he brought home one more VCR that he was sure he could fix. So what if three nonworking models stood precariously on top of their living room TV?

"Faye Beth is having a little trouble with her hormones," he offered other diners when down at the Wild Flour Café, after he had helped himself to a bite of her Spanish meatloaf, then her crowder peas, and finally her garlic mashed potatoes, she stuck him with her fork and drew blood. (He, not really hungry, had only ordered iced tea.)

Couples residing in a city might have chosen to visit a counselor. But in Ella Louise? Folks don't take kindly to the idea of having their heads shrunk. So Faye Beth and Harvey just limped along.

Until the day Harvey let his goats get into Faye Beth's rose garden. That was the thing that got on her last nerve.

Harvey, arriving home from work an hour late that afternoon, at first didn't remember leaving the gate open. He supposed he could have accidentally done so early that morning when he went out to the storage room to retrieve an old issue of *Field and Stream* so he would have something to read during his lunch break. With a sinking feeling at the sight he saw when he arrived home, Harvey knew that's what most likely had happened.

What Harvey saw was the remains of Faye Beth's rose garden—her pride and joy. Faye Beth had babied those roses same as he babied his goats; he'd swear he heard her talking to them when she thought he wasn't listening. Her garden boasted roses of every color, size, and variety. Faye Beth researched roses, read about roses, even sent off to the UPS man for roses. Once a week, she cut some roses and took them down to the elderly folks at the rest home. From the spent blossoms she made rose potpourri. When he had a cold, she made him something called rose-hip tea.

But Faye Beth wouldn't be doing any of that for a while. The sight that greeted Harvey when he arrived home on that day was a bunch of almost-chewed-to-the-ground bushes and a yard full of happy goats with rose-scented breath. Pals of Harvey, the herd raised their heads in unison and called "baa" when they saw him get out of the truck, as if to say "We've all had a *very* good day. How about you?"

Well, Harvey's day was about to get worse. He started to sweat, because not even one of Faye Beth's rose bushes was left unchewed. And where was Faye Beth, anyway? The Chevy in the driveway told him that she'd already arrived home. Was she in the house? Had she somehow not seen the goats in her garden?

Then a movement on the roof of the trailer caught his eye. Faye Beth was up there, but because her back was to him, the only thing

Harvey could see from his spot on the ground was Faye Beth's red-Capri-pants-clad bottom.

"Faye Beth?"

She didn't hear him.

"Honey?"

She didn't hear him because she was busy.

"Sugar?"

Busy busting a hole in his precious roof.

Janet had forgotten about her potholes and Rochelle her tan.

"Faye Beth, you have got to be lying!" said Janet.

"You knocked a hole in your own roof?" said Rochelle. "For real?"

"Sure did," said Faye Beth. "When I saw what Harvey's goats had done to my roses, well, something just came over me. Next thing I knew, I was up on that roof, whacking away at the shingles."

"What did Harvey do?" asked Janet.

"He brought me a glass of tea."

"No!"

"He did. When I saw him coming up the ladder, trying real hard not to spill it—he had fixed it with lemon just the way I like it—well, I realized that my Harvey was a pretty brave man."

"Brave?"

"Honey, I had a sledgehammer in my hand."

"What did you do then?"

"Well, first off I drank the tea Harvey had fixed.

Then finished knocking that hole in the roof. After that, I climbed down, went into the house, and fried up some steak for us to have for supper."

"Harvey didn't say anything?"

"Not a word, except could I please pass the black pepper. I suppose there wasn't much he thought he could say. Pretty soon, he went in to take his bath, and I got out my Bible to do my evening reading. You know what verse I came to?"

"What?"

"Proverbs fourteen and one. I wasn't the only one swinging a sledgehammer that day. The Lord had one too. Hit me right between the eyes. Right there in black and white were these words: 'The wise woman builds her house, but with her own hands the foolish one tears hers down.' All of a sudden all the hurt and anger I felt just drained away, and all I felt was shame. I knew that I had been one foolish woman for many, many days. When Harvey got out of the tub, I was waiting for him with a big bowl of ice cream. I told him that I was sorry, and he told me that I wasn't the only one to blame and that he was sorry too. We vowed then and there that we would try harder to get along."

"What a story!" said Rochelle. "I guess after you made up and all that, Harvey fixed the hole in the roof. Did you get up there and help him?" asked Rochelle.

"No, I didn't. Hole's still there."

"Just a small hole then," said Janet.

"Big enough to drive a riding lawn mower through."

"Really?"

"Then how come Harvey hasn't fixed it?"

"I asked him not to. You see, Harvey and I are both plagued with short memories. Even though we were real sorry about everything that day, knowing us, it wouldn't have been any time before we were back to our old selfish ways. This way, every time we come home and every time we leave home, neither one of us can help but see the roof of our house and think about how we nearly tore our marriage apart for nothing more than not paying attention to what our actions were doing to each other. So that's why if you ever drive out to see our place, you'll see a big old hunk tore out of our roof."

Most couples rely on wedding rings, old photos, or some other romantic momento to remind them of the vows they've taken to love and to honor until death do them part. Faye Beth and Harvey are the only couple I know who have chosen hacked-up plywood and missing shingles to do the same thing.

But you know, it works. Whenever I'm in Ella Louise, I make it a point to drive out to their house. If I've been acting testy with my own dear husband—which, given my high-strung temperament, is too often the case—one look at their house and I'm back on track.

Yes. I agree with Faye Beth on this. Sometimes a gaping hole is best let be.

12

Butter Up

Six months after her husband, Joe's, sudden death from a heart attack, Bessie Bishop paid cash for a house in Ella Louise. It was a frame house, a story and a half, white with dark-blue trim, on a street one block south of downtown. She picked it from among all the ones she looked at because it had a porch swing and a birdbath.

For all of their married life, Bessie and Joe had called various large cities home. First Los Angeles, then Boston, Pittsburgh, and finally Houston. Joe's job as a corporate executive required the moves, and Bessie, a nurse, never had any trouble finding part-time work wherever they lived. But while they'd made the best of those years—enjoying concerts, plays, and nice restaurants—Bessie and Joe had looked forward to the day when they could retire and move to a small town. Joe had always said that when you took away his shirt and tie, he was really a country boy at heart. When the time came, he planned to trade in his Buick for a Ford pickup truck.

"Bess, I want us to move someplace where I can spend my Saturday mornings leaning back on a bench with the other old men—you know, in front of the drugstore or the courthouse. I want to hear fat lies about women and war," said Joe. "Sugar, I'm warning you. I aim to become a codger in my old age. I may learn to spit. And how about you?" he teased. "You gonna take up crochet?"

When Joe was two years from retiring, they had begun looking around at prospective locations, wondering what it would be like to live in this area or that one, weighing the plusses and minuses of various small communities. It was two months before Joe died when the pair of them, on a weekend jaunt, had come upon Ella Louise.

"Nice place," Bessie remembered Joe saying. "This little town might be the one. It's got a grocery store, a library, and a pharmacy. The folks seem friendly, and it's less than two hours from Houston. What do you think, hon?"

She'd thought the town was just right. So much so, that even though Joe was gone, she was still heading toward Ella Louise.

On moving day, Bessie's sons, Leland and Roy, nearly killed themselves trying to move their mother's things. Getting her antique player piano into the house proved to be almost more than they could do. Even after backing the rented U-Haul up close to the front door, the two struggled to hoist the thing up the house's five front steps.

"Lands!" said Leland to Roy. "If I'd known this thing was so heavy, I'd have insisted she hire a mover. I'm not sure we're gonna make it."

"You know Mother. Anything to save a dime." Roy stretched his lower back. "This piano's heavy all right, but remember, we've still got the hide-a-bed ahead of us."

"Reckon it'll be as bad?"

"You know it."

While her sons were at the new house in Ella Louise, straining themselves with the heavy stuff, Bessie was in Houston, packing up her kitchen, her hall closets, and her backyard storage building. She was also fretting about her cat, Baby. "I feel silly worrying about a cat," she confided to her long-time neighbor, Sandy, who had come over to help her pack. "I've never been one to carry on about a pet, but ever since Joe died, Baby's been a comfort to me. I don't want to lose her, but they say cats don't take to a move very well."

"Couldn't you just keep her inside?"

"Maybe I will for a few days, but she's always been an inside-outside cat. Mostly outside. Last year, when we had that long spell of cold weather, I got her a litter box so she wouldn't have to go outside. Stubborn thing refused to use it. When she wanted outside, she'd go stand by the door and meow. She's a funny little cat. Pretty opinionated. I'm afraid she'll run away from the new place."

Sandy thought for a moment. "My grand-mother loved cats. She had three. I remember that when I was a little girl and she and my grandpa moved, she rubbed butter on all of their feet."

"Butter? What's that supposed to do?" Bessie asked.

"I'm not exactly sure, but I think it has something to do with the cats concentrating so hard on licking the butter off that they forget they've moved. Now, for it to work, you're supposed to rub the butter real good—lots of it—between the cat's toes. Way I remember my grandmother telling it, by the time the cat manages to lick all the butter off, they're supposed to have come to think of the new place as their home and not try to run away."

"I never heard of such a thing. I guess it's worth a try." Bessie looked over at Baby, asleep in an heirloom crystal fruit bowl. "Wonder if Parkay margarine would work. I've let my pantry and refrigerator get down to almost nothing. I'm out of real butter."

"I don't think I'd take a chance," said Sandy. "I've got butter in my fridge. I'll run and get you a stick."

When Leland and Roy came back with the U-Haul to get the rest of her things, Bessie, with Sandy's help, had gotten everything packed and ready to go. She'd also buttered Baby and closed her in her carrier. In the process, she'd gotten butter all over herself, but she was careful to clean off the evidence so that neither of her sons would know what she'd done; they would likely make fun. It didn't take them long to haul the last of the boxes and smaller pieces of furniture into the truck.

Sandy hugged her. "I'm not going to stay and watch you leave. It's too hard. You know that I'm here if you need me." She tried not to cry. "Call me."

"I will."

"Okay, Mother," said Leland, "this is it. Ready?"

"Why don't you ride with me in the truck and let Leland drive your car?" said Roy. "I figured we'd get down the road about half an hour, and then we can all stop and get a bite to eat."

"No," said Bessie. "I want to go by myself. You boys go on. Me and Baby are going to be a few minutes behind you."

"We can wait, Mom. Me and Roy are in no hurry."

The boys didn't understand. Bessie and Joe had spent their last ten years together in the house, but neither of her sons had ever lived there. They missed their dad, of course, and on this their mother's moving day, they were both thinking of him. But as for the house? Its walls held sentimental meaning for her, but not for them. Bessie patted Roy on the back. "Son, I'm fine. Really. I just need a minute, that's all. You boys go on. See if you can't get my washer and dryer hooked up tonight, will you? That'd be a big help. And careful with that biggest box. It's got your great-grandmother's china inside."

When Leland and Roy finally climbed into the truck, Bessie moved from the front yard to the middle of the street. The truck was a difficult vehicle to back up, so she helped by motioning Roy, who was driving, to steer a bit more to the right and then a wee bit further to the left. When he finally was backed out and headed the right way, he rolled down the window.

"You're coming along soon, right Mom? I don't want you driving by yourself after dark."

"Honey, don't worry. I'll only be a few minutes behind you. Promise," Bessie assured.

She stood in the street and waved as the truck chugged to the end of the block. She watched it pause at the stop sign, saw the turn signal flash, and then watched the truck make the turn. Even after it was gone from her sight, Bessie stood rooted in the street. She had to will herself to move.

She was surprised at how much she longed to

delay her leaving. All day long she had been anticipating and dreading this moment—the one when she would close the door to the house, get into her car, and drive to Ella Louise. Though she was sure moving was what she wanted to do, was the right thing to do, she couldn't believe that the time to do it was actually here.

Inside the house, she moved from room to room, noticing the worn spots in the carpet and the smudges on the walls and woodwork. Had they been there all along? She hadn't noticed. If only she had more time to clean the carpet, the walls, and the woodwork too! Tears filled her eyes. "It's only a house," she told herself. "Brick and mortar and carpet and tile."

But memories too.

In the master bedroom, Bessie leaned against a bare wall and thought of all the nights she'd slept curled against Joe's warm back. She remembered how embarrassed she'd been when she learned that she snored. "Why didn't you tell me?" she'd asked Joe after spending the weekend at a women's church retreat. "Sandy and Gracie were my roommates, and they teased me something terrible. Both of them said I sounded like a grizzly bear in hibernation. They told me they couldn't sleep for all the noise I made. The second night, I saw them sneak around and stuff their ears with some cotton that Sandy dug out of her bottle of vitamin C. Honey, tell me. Do I keep *you* awake?

Because if I do, I'll start sleeping in the other bedroom."

Joe had patted her on the knee. "No. Of course you don't keep me awake, and no, you're not going to sleep in the other room."

"But the snoring?"

"It's not so loud."

"Really?"

"Really."

"How long have I been doing it?"

"I dunno. Couple of years? Maybe more. I kind of like it."

"Joe! I'm serious here. Don't give me a hard time."

"I am being serious. The sound of your snoring is comforting to me. On the nights that you don't snore, I have a hard time falling asleep. I'm so used to it that when you're gone overnight, it's too quiet. I lie awake forever before I fall asleep."

A dear, dear man. Joe always did have a different way of looking at things.

Bessie blew her nose. Then she moved from the bedroom to the living room. She stood there for a long while, nose pressed to the sliding glass door, and gazed out at the backyard. The apple trees Joe babied all year long looked like they would yield a good crop of fruit this year.

She recalled the time when, relaxing in the hammock, she opened her eyes from her Sunday afternoon nap to see something very odd growing in the apple tree overhead. It was an . . . well, it couldn't be, but it sure did look like an . . . an . . . an orange. An orange growing on a branch in the middle of a bunch of nearly-ripe apples. Bessie rubbed her eyes and struggled to sit up. When she saw that it really *was* an orange, she nearly tipped herself out onto the ground.

Not until she had gotten out the ladder, positioned it under the tree, and climbed to the third step did she hear Joe snickering. From his post around the corner of the house, he had eased to where he was now, at the foot of the ladder. "Whatcha doin', dear?" he asked with feigned innocence. "Bit early to be plucking apples, don't you think? I don't believe they're ripe yet."

"Joe," Bessie said. "Look." She pointed to the orange, still out of her reach. "Isn't that odd?"

"What the—?" he said. "Why, that looks like a . . . well, like an orange growing in our apple tree? Bess! We better call the county agent. Shoot! We'd best call the *National Enquirer*!"

Bessie was inclined to agree with him until she looked down and saw that he was struggling to keep a straight face. While she'd been asleep, fifty-five-year-old Joe had climbed the tree and tied the orange to a branch, for no other reason than to see what she'd do.

That Joe! He had never lost his childlike streak. Kids loved him. Bessie opened one of the kitchen drawers and found half a piece of Big

Red gum. She unwrapped it and popped it in her mouth. One of the reasons kids had liked Joe so much was that he always carried gum in his pockets for them.

Joe and Bessie were the teachers of their church's Wednesday night four-year-olds Bible class. Early on, they worked out a system. Bessie made snacks, led the children in singing songs, and prepared the craft. Joe's job was to teach the lesson—which he did with great creativity and aplomb.

Joe did not believe that a bunch of four-year-olds could be expected to sit in little chairs and listen to a story read out of the teacher's handbook. No way. Though he had no training in teaching children, he was of the strong opinion that kids learned best by doing, by getting their hands on stuff, by acting out whatever it was they were supposed to learn.

Which made for some messy, noisy, out-of-the-ordinary Wednesday nights.

Take, for instance, the week that the children learned about the story of David and Goliath. A bit wary of what Joe might decide to do, Bessie pointed out to him that the teacher's packet had some very nice flannel-graph figures to use.

But Joe had something else in mind.

Before class, he taped sheets of butcher paper together to make a strip more than six feet long and three feet wide. He had never been very good with sticky stuff, and by the time he got the project all done he had used almost the whole roll of tape. After telling the children about how young David had killed Goliath with five stones (in a wee bit too much gory detail, Bessie thought), he put the paper on the floor, lay on top of it, and directed the children to draw around him with black markers. Bessie helped them, and only a few marks got on his socks and (oops!) in his gray hair. Once they'd made the tracing—of him as the giant, you see— Joe rose from the floor, rolled up their creation, and stuck it under his arm. Then he lined up the children and marched the troop of ten toward the outside door.

"Shhh!" he whispered as the children made their way through the hallways. "Everybody on tiptoe!" The deacon in charge of education was never all that sure about Joe's unconventional teaching techniques. Joe had come to the conclusion that as far as deacons go, begging for forgiveness was easier than asking for permission.

Joe led the children to the playground behind the church. "No, we're not going to play. At least not yet. Bessie," he said as the children watched, their eyes wide with wonder, "I'm climbing to the top of the slide. When I get up there, you hand me the tape and the paper. Okay?"

Bessie had no idea what it was he planned to do. "Careful, Joe," she said.

He climbed up like a monkey, then Bessie handed him his stuff. Joe taped the tracing to the top of the slide. Then he got down.

"Remember how David threw rocks at the giant?" he primed the kids. "That's what we're going to do too! See the man hanging from the slide? He's big isn't he? He's a giant, like Goliath. We get to be like David. Everybody got a rock?"

Oh, they surely did.

"Good! Now let's all get the giant!"

Joe's lesson was a big hit. Several hits, in fact. There are few things that four-year-olds, especially boys, enjoy doing more than throwing rocks. There was only one glitch in that night's lesson. Some of the children's mothers got a bit upset when, in response to the question "What did you do in Bible class?" their little darlings confessed with glee, "We went outside and threw rocks at Mr. Bishop!"

It didn't take long for Bessie's stick of gum to lose its flavor. She spit it out. She ended her final walk-through in the living room. Baby, who was sitting by the front door in her carrier, heard Bessie's footsteps. She began to wail. "Ready to go, are you?" Bessie said. "Guess it's time." She picked up her purse, then remembered the keys. Just as she'd promised the house's new owners, she laid them on the mantel above the fireplace.

On the threshold, just before stepping out the front door, Bessie turned around and took one last look. From her spot in the entrance hall, she could see past the living room and into part of the kitchen and breakfast nook. Looking the other way, she could see the hallway that led to the master bedroom. "Bye, house," she whispered.

Nothing but quiet.

Then Bessie stepped out and closed the door behind her. She walked to her car, set Baby's carrier on the floor behind her seat, got in, backed out of the driveway, and did not look back.

Leland and Roy had indeed gotten Bessie's washer and dryer hooked up. They'd also gone to the store to buy milk, bread, toilet paper, and lightbulbs. Bessie guessed that a person's needs didn't get much more basic than that. Once they got all of her furniture moved to where she wanted it, both boys offered to spend the night with her. They thought it best that she have company on her first night in the new house.

Bessie thought not. No, they should go on home. She was fine. Really.

And she was.

After her sons left, Bessie, a night owl, got busy unpacking boxes. She decided she would get as much of her kitchen stuff put away as she could. Being able to make toast and coffee in the morning would be good.

Where to put what? It was hard to decide. She'd been working for more than an hour when, suddenly, she gasped. Baby! Still in the car!

"You poor thing! I'm sorry! Did you think I was going to leave you out here all night?"

Baby was not a happy cat. When Bessie let her out of the carrier, the first thing Baby did was dash across the room and duck under the hide-a-bed, her buttery paws leaving greasy marks on the carpet as she ran. Poor thing. Bessie knew that Baby must be thirsty. Hungry too. She lay down on her stomach so she could see Baby under the sofa. "Here, kitty. Here, kitty. Kitty, kitty, kitty."

Baby didn't budge. Her response to Bessie's pleading was to hunker herself into a corner and stare out with unblinking, frightened yellow eyes.

Nothing Bessie did could convince her to come out. After trying and trying, Bessie finally gave up and went back to her unpacking. Not until a good two hours had passed did Baby finally slink from her hiding place to sniff at the bowl of food poured for her. Cautiously, she took a bite. When Bessie approached her, Baby paused to cast an accusing look in her direction. *One false move,* the cat's expression said, *and I'll head for cover—just you watch!*

But as she ate, Baby calmed down. "There now," Bessie said, "that's better. You're going to be okay. I am too. It's going to take us both a while to get used to our new place." Baby relaxed and even let herself be petted. When she did, Bessie scooped Baby up in her arms. Until Baby appeared to act like this house in Ella Louise was her home, Bessie decided that it was best that she stay in the utility room, which was prepared with fresh water, a soft blanket for a bed, and a litter box.

Insulted at being confined, however, Baby howled all night, pausing intermittently to lick at the butter between her furry toes.

She howled most of the next day.

And the next night too.

On the third day, Bessie let her out to roam the house, hopeful that she might begin to feel at home. But doing so did not help Baby's miserable state. Instead of hiding under the furniture, she took to standing at the back door, wailing to be let out.

Bessie gave in. She opened up the back door and the second that Baby spotted the open door, she dashed out.

From the doorway, Bessie stood and watched her beloved kitty trot south. When Bessie called her, Baby neither paused nor looked back. Without a doubt, this little feline had a definite destination in mind.

For several days, Bessie held out hope that Baby would be back. When she got up in the morning, she unlocked and opened her back door, hoping to find Baby waiting for her breakfast. But she didn't. A whole week passed, then two, and finally three with no sign of Baby. Since she'd heard of animals trekking miles and miles to get back home, Bessie mentioned Baby's disappearance to her old neighbor, Sandy.

"No, Bessie, I haven't seen her. But I promise I'll keep watch. Still—I can't imagine that she'd make it all the way back here. Can you? I'm sure sorry that the butter thing didn't work."

Bessie missed her kitty, especially in the evening, when she thought a lot about Joe. But as she got herself settled into life in Ella Louise, she found a lot to keep herself busy, and that helped. Besides getting the house set up like she wanted it, Bessie started planting a garden and she joined the Gentle Thimble Quilting Club, after the ladies assured her that it was okay that she didn't know how to quilt. They'd be happy to teach her.

Soon after she moved in, Bessie met her neighbor, a friendly widower named Crow Buxley. He was gentle and kind, and as far as Bessie could tell, harmless enough. She found it helpful to have a man she could call on when she needed help with her yard or her house.

But still there were times when Bessie was so lonely that she wondered if perhaps she should have stayed in Houston, where at least the house reminded her of Joe. In Ella Louise, there was nothing of his and that made her sad.

Bessie had lived in Ella Louise for four months when she first spotted the opossum in her front yard. At first she wasn't sure what it was because the thing scurried out of sight and ducked under the hedges before she got a good look. But then, over the next two days, she spotted it three more times. When she began to hear fierce scratchings and carryings on under her house, she asked around and found out that this was indeed a big opossum year. She was told that opossums were notorious for tearing up a person's yard and rooting up shrubs and flowers. She needed to get rid of the animal.

When she told Crow about her problem, he brought over a trap. Bessie didn't want to do anything cruel. What if the opossum was a mother? What if she had babies?

"Don't worry," Crow assured. "This kind of trap won't hurt 'em. Scare 'em maybe, but that's all. If we catch us one, I'll take it out to the woods and let it go. Won't be no harm done."

That eased Bessie's mind.

So four evenings in a row, Crow came over to set and bait the trap. And four mornings in a row, he came back to find that the bait had been taken, but no critter caught. Finally, on the fifth morning, Bessie looked out her kitchen window and, though she was a distance away, saw that this time there was something caught inside the trap. Something black and white.

Black and white?

"Crow," she said when after seven rings he finally answered the phone, "did I wake you? I'm sorry. It's early, I know, but could you come over real quick? I'm afraid that we may have caught us a skunk."

"Sure, I'll come. Soon as I get my pants—I mean as soon as I get my shoes on."

Bessie didn't dare go outside for fear that she would stir the skunk up, and he would do what skunks do. So she kept watch on its movements from her kitchen window. Best she could tell, the animal kept sticking its foot out between the wires of the cage. That was odd. She sure hoped that Crow would know what to do.

He did.

When Crow pulled up in his truck, he didn't come directly in the house. Instead, he went to check the trap. Bessie was still watching from the window when he motioned for her to come outside.

She went to the door and stood there in the frame, not sure that she should go out.

"Come on," he called. "You need to see this."

"No thanks."

"Come look," coaxed Crow.

She eased down two steps.

"Bessie, your skunk isn't a skunk at all. We've

caught us a cat. Black and white like a skunk, but just a pretty little cat."

A cat? Baby? It couldn't be!

But it was. Baby had lost weight and her coat was dull, but there was no doubt. She had come back!

"You mean this is your cat?" said Crow. "The one that ran off right after you moved here? Bessie, that's been what, three months?"

She couldn't believe it either. When the two of them sat in her kitchen, watching Baby gobble down her second can of tuna, Bessie said, "Crow, when this little kitty left, she headed straight south. She was so unhappy here and so determined to leave that I just gave up and let her go. When a week had passed with no sign of her, I knew she wasn't coming back. What I figured was that she got killed trying to get back to our old house. What I hoped was that she got tired and took up with someone kind along the way. I never, ever expected her back."

Baby finished her breakfast, gave herself a bath, yawned, and settled herself down for a nap on a sunny spot on the floor.

"She looks like she's planning on staying around for a while," said Crow.

"Yes. She does."

"How about you?"

Bessie looked up.

"You planning on staying around?"

"Yes. I am."

"Good. Glad to hear it." Crow rose to go. "You make a good neighbor. I'd hate to see you leave."

"Sandy? This is Bessie. How are you? Good. Good. Listen, you'll never believe it. Baby came home. That old wives' tale about putting butter on a cat's paws—well, it's true. Uh-huh. Really. It worked on Baby."

And from the contentment that shows on her face, I'd say it worked on Bessie too.

13

A Pinch of Sugar

"When I grow up, I'm going to be a missionary. I'll go to Africa to teach the little children about Jesus," six-year-old Tiny told her parents.

"When I grow up, I'm going to be a nurse and join the Air Force and fly on an airplane to take care of injured soldiers," Tiny told her third-grade teacher.

"When I grow up, I'm going to be a famous singer. I'll travel all around the world and wear shiny dresses and have my own makeup woman," Tiny told her best friend in junior high.

"Housewife" is what grown-up Tiny Tinker prints on the "occupation" line whenever she fills out a form. Regrets? No. She and her Alfred, who is now halfway through his third two-year term as Ella Louise's mayor, have been married for thirty-two years. All but one of those has been good.

Alfred and Tiny's fifth year of marriage broke their hearts. Their only child, Tammy, was fifteen months old at the time. With blond curls and blue eyes, Tammy was the prettiest baby that folks had ever seen. She was what the town's old wives called a good baby, one that smiled all the time and would sing and play in her crib for more than an hour before calling to be gotten up. Her pleasant, quiet disposition was likely what caused Tiny to lose track of her for a few minutes on a sunny summer day.

Tiny was peeling potatoes at the sink on that day, looking out the window, humming and daydreaming, as she was prone to do. Tammy played at her feet—for how long, Tiny can't recall. After a time, Tiny realized that Tammy wasn't with her in the kitchen anymore. So she wiped her hands on a tea towel and went looking for her crawling child. "Tammy," she remembers calling, "Where are you?" She found Tammy in the mudroom, just off the kitchen. "What are you doing? What's that you've got in your mouth? Plums? You sneaky little girl. Are they good?"

Tammy had helped herself to the contents of a half-bushel basket of ripe plums. Tiny thought she looked cute on her knees beside the basket, plum juice running down the sides of her face, her hands sticky and her little dress a mess. "You little imp! We better put you in the bath."

That night, Tammy got sick. Her little tummy swelled up and she began to run a fever. Tiny took her to the doctor early the next morning, and he took one look at the baby and told Tiny to take her to the hospital. The next day, Tammy died. It was anyone's guess as to exactly what had happened, but Tammy's baby doctor believed that the plums Tammy ate, specifically the seeds inside the plums, caused an obstruction in her little bowel. At the time, there was nothing that could be done.

Alfred and Tiny grieved for their little girl. Everyone told them that they needed to have another baby, but though they tried and tried, Tiny never again conceived.

Many couples that lose a child end up losing each other too.

That didn't happen to Alfred and Tiny. If anything, their loss made them cling to each other like never before.

Many mothers who lose a child forfeit every bit of joy in their lives.

Not Tiny. While the raw place in her heart never went away, and while the sight of a newborn calf nuzzling its mother or dolls in a toy-store window sometimes made her flinch, losing Tammy somehow made her softer, more tender, more acutely aware of life's beauty than she had been before.

Alfred and Tiny are what folks in Ella Louise call salt of the earth. Tiny is blessed with such a kind face and warm heart that no matter where she is—at a church social, a ballgame, or even on a bench at the mall—children who have never laid eyes on her before crawl up in her lap when they want to go to sleep.

Alfred has worked with the Boy Scouts for years, and he helps out at their camp every summer. Year before last, he arrived at camp without his blood pressure medicine, so he called Tiny and asked her to bring it up to him. When she arrived, a group of the youngest campers was standing nearby. Within minutes, the whole homesick, mosquito-bitten bunch was standing beside her. Just standing there. They were all missing their mothers, and Tiny was the next best thing.

Kids know when someone is good and kind.

Which sort of breaks your heart.

On the first anniversary of her marriage, Tiny's best friend, Sugar Fry, tore open the card that her sweetie had proudly laid on her breakfast plate. Its flowery verse brought tears to her eyes —until she saw how her beloved had signed the card.

Sincerely, Millard Fry
May 13, 1959

"Millard!" She began to cry.

"What? You don't like the card?" It had cost two dollars. How could she not like it?

Millard and Sugar's marriage started out on the rocks. The first thing Millard did after he and his bride moved into their new house was dig up all the grass in the front yard and put in a rock garden. It took him all day. As soon as he was done with the front, he started on the back.

That made Sugar cry too.

Which puzzled Millard. After all, they didn't own a lawnmower, and rock gardens didn't have to be mowed. Right? Made sense to him.

So for pretty much the first six months of their marriage, Millard made Sugar cry. Honestly, he couldn't help it. Raised by his daddy and an uncle—he'd had no mama—Millard didn't have a clue how to live with a woman.

Millard nearly drove Sugar crazy with his muddy-shoed stompings through the house, his loud voice, and his constant need to be on the go. He was so energetic that in an effort to calm him down before he wore her out, Sugar began to make his morning coffee half decaf.

Which, of course, did no good.

Early on in their marriage, Millard and Sugar decided to start a family. When they were blessed with their daughter, Shonda, Millard calmed down—for a couple of days. Restless, he still needed to be busy, to be working all the time.

"Daddy go work," was Shonda's first sentence.

"Yes, baby. Daddy go work," said Sugar.

It was not until Shonda grew up and gave them a darling granddaughter, Millie Tonette, that Millard began to mellow. Maybe it was his age, or maybe it was the spell that only a granddaughter knows how to cast. For whatever reason, every year after Millie's birth, Millard became calmer, more tender-hearted, and more sentimental about everything.

Millard changed so much that sometimes Sugar wondered to herself, *Who is this man? What has he done with my husband?*

Sugar read somewhere—might have been in *Reader's Digest*—that there are these special hairs that grow on peoples' brains. These hairs are what make folks care about home and family, domestic stuff. Women have really long brain hairs when they are young, which makes them want to nurture their families, to take care of their kids and their houses. Men, on the other hand, have short brain hairs, so all they want to do is stay on the run—to their jobs, to the lake, to the golf course—and be anywhere but home.

Well, according to the article, women's brain hairs start to break off about the time when their kids are grown. That's when they feel the need to get out of the house, explore the world, and be on the run like the men.

Which would be a good thing, except for the fact that that's the time when men's brain hairs finally start to grow.

That, best as Sugar could tell, was what happened to her and Millard.

By the time Millard hit fifty-five, all he wanted to do was play with the grandbaby, invite folks over for dominos, sit down and eat home-cooked meals (the kind that required Sugar to spend long hours in the kitchen), and watch *Wheel of Fortune.*

But when Sugar hit fifty-five, she realized that she was sick of cooking. She hung up her apron and got herself a job. She hired someone to clean her house once a week, discovered Hamburger Helper and frozen potpies, and began researching vacation spots on the Internet.

Poor Millard didn't know what to do. Had Sugar gone crazy or something? The woman wanted to stay gone all the time. Terribly confused, he began bringing her all kinds of gifts—flowers, an omelet pan, a bread machine, a birdbath.

One day, over lunch, Sugar shared with Tiny her and Millard's marital shift and the compromises they were both having to make.

"Not been easy for either one of us. And all because of those brain hairs. That's where I lay the blame. Growing. Breaking off. Long. Then short. It's no wonder that sometimes I feel like I'm just one long split end. Kind of makes you wonder if God screwed our heads on wrong."

Tiny giggled. "Sugar! Shush! You can't be talking about God that way."

"I know. I know." She looked heavenward. "God, I'm sorry." Then she looked back at Tiny. "You planning on eating the rest of your pie?"

It was Tiny's second piece. "You can have it." She slid her plate across the table. "Got any plans for Thursday?"

"No."

"Me either. Let's drive down to Houston. Make a day of it. Go to a couple of museums, have lunch. Maybe shop."

"Uh-uh," Sugar said. "I'm not going with you to any museums."

"Come on. I promise I'll be good. At least I'll try." But both of them knew it was no use. Tiny never could keep her hands to herself. When she was in a museum, she got so caught up in the interesting things that she was compelled, almost trancelike, to reach out and touch—a sculpture, a tapestry, a gilded egg.

How many museums had Tiny been kicked out of? More than a dozen. She knew from experience that some displays—there was no way to tell which ones—were equipped with silent alarms. Over and over, in response to her having handled some priceless, irreplaceable object, armed guards appeared out of nowhere to escort her out the door and into her car.

Sheesh. It wasn't like she was going to steal anything.

Tiny and Sugar go way back. They have been friends for thirty years. When they were newlyweds, the two couples were neighbors. Since both of their husbands spent long hours working, Tiny and Sugar kept each other company. On Mondays they cleaned Tiny's house. On Wednesdays they cleaned Sugar's. Tiny hated to iron but was a great seamstress. Sugar liked to iron, but once got so frustrated while trying to make a blouse that she cut the thing to ribbons. So they decided that Tiny would do Sugar's sewing and Sugar would do Tiny's ironing.

Which worked out great.

In those early years, neither couple had much money. While no one went hungry, many nights dinner was beans and cornbread or a can of chicken noodle soup and American cheese on toast. One December day, Tiny's daddy stopped by and surprised her and Alfred with a turkey. She cooked it, they ate it, and she boiled the bones for soup. They enjoyed the soup so much that once Tiny was done with the bones, she handed them over to Sugar so she could use them to make soup for her and Millard.

What good soup that was.

Alfred and Tiny wanted to wait until he got out of school before they started having kids. To do so only made sense.

But Millard and Sugar weren't in agreement on that issue. Sugar said that now that she was married, she aimed to start having kids. So what if she and Millard didn't have much money? She wanted a baby!

It was "Visit the Shut-Ins" day with the ladies of the church when Tiny and Sugar dropped Sugar's specimen off at the doctor's office. "You can call in two hours, honey," Sugar was told by the nurse. "We should have the results for you then."

Who would have guessed that when the two hours were up, they would be in the middle of visiting old Mrs. Crutchfield? Tiny kept looking at her watch. She motioned to Sugar when it was time.

"Mrs. Crutchfield, may I please use your phone?" asked Sugar.

"Is it long distance?"

"No, ma'am."

"All right. It's in the kitchen."

As they sipped their tea in the living room, Tiny and Mrs. Crutchfield heard Sugar scream. Then Sugar dropped the phone and rushed in to them. "Can you believe it? I'm going to have a baby!"

But soon after she received the joyful news, Sugar began fretting over where her baby would sleep when it was born. She didn't have a crib or cradle, and she and Millard had no money to buy one. It was December, and Christmas carols were playing on all the radio stations. "Poor baby. Just like the little Lord Jesus. No crib for a bed. Not even a manger."

Then Tiny had an idea. She took one of the drawers from her and Alfred's dresser and fixed it up into a pretty place for Sugar's baby to sleep. She cut up one of her ruffled dresses to make a sweet little pillow, used stuffing from one of the throw pillows off of her couch to make a mattress, and pieced together a coverlet. By the time she got through fixing up that dresser drawer, she and Sugar agreed that except for the hardware (which they both thought best not to remove since the drawer would go back in the dresser once the baby got too big) it was almost as pretty as a store-bought bassinet.

Tiny was always doing something sweet.

She was also always eating too many sweets. Which, combined with her family's medical history, was not a good thing. In her early forties, Tiny's diabetes, which she'd had since her late twenties, got worse. In her late forties, her kidneys began to show wear. By her fiftieth birthday, she was told she'd likely be on dialysis within the year.

"How many hours a day?" asked Sugar.

"Four."

"Once a week?"

"Three," said Tiny.

"That's awful. There's no other option?" said Sugar.

"Nope. Down the line, a kidney transplant, maybe—but the docs won't even talk about that

201

until both these kidneys of mine completely tucker out."

Which they did by the end of that year. So Tiny was put on dialysis. Her skin took on a grayish hue, she lost her energy, and though she tried to fake it, anyone who knew her was aware that she felt awful almost all of the time. The dialysis would keep her alive, but it was a poor, poor substitute for a functioning kidney.

Talk of a transplant commenced. There were two kinds of kidneys one could get—one from a cadaver and one from a living donor. A kidney from a living donor would be best.

Alfred hated seeing his wife so sick. At an early visit with Tiny's doctor, he told the man that he was ready to give Tiny a kidney. They could take it from him tomorrow. What exactly did they need him to do? Sign some papers, get some tests done? Alfred rolled up his sleeve. They could start right now.

But there was more to it than that. After the results of some tests came back, Alfred was told that his kidney would not work. Incompatible? He and Tiny? He was devastated. What now?

Since Tiny had no living relative healthy enough to qualify for even preliminary donor testing, she was put on a list to receive a cadaver kidney—one from a healthy person who had died.

How long would she have to wait?

No way to know.

Months? Years?

Could be.

Six months into the dialysis, Sugar was bent over Tiny's feet, painting her toenails a pretty pink. She did it every week. Out of the blue, she asked, "What about me? You think mine would work?"

"Your what?" Tiny had been daydreaming about Chinese food, which, because of its high salt content, she could not have.

"My kidney. You think my kidney would work for you?"

Tiny didn't speak for a long time. The polish on her toes was dry before she finally said, "You want to see?"

"Yes, I do. Millard and I've been talking about it for the past three months. Me? I've been thinking about it since the day you found out that you and Alfred weren't a match."

"It's a big, big deal to give a kidney," said Tiny.

"I know. I've been reading up on it."

"So you really want to see."

"I do."

"It's going to hurt."

"So? My mama always told me you can't make an omelet without breaking eggs."

"You're a big baby when it comes to pain."

"I hear they give you drugs."

"They're going to be taking a part of your own body away."

"Not a very big part."

Tiny gave her a look.

"Compared to the size of the rest of me, no more than a pinch is the way I'm looking at it. A pinch of Sugar. That, my friend, is what I think you need. It's what I want to give you. Okay? Now, give me your hand. You want the same color as what I've put on your toes?"

Preliminary tests showed that Sugar looked like a good match. A really good match. Before they would know for sure, doctors did more extensive testing, blood work, X-rays, even a long psychological exam.

"Took me an hour and a half to do the written part, and then I had to talk to the head shrinker for another hour," Sugar reported to Tiny after she'd taken the test. "Took 'em that long to figure out that I'm sane—at least sane as anyone can be who is planning on giving away a vital organ! Wonder which one they'll take, my right or my left?"

Three months later, their husbands drove them to the hospital. Despite Tiny and Sugar's protests, they were assigned separate rooms on different floors. "Yes," they were both informed after they'd sipped clear liquid dinners, "you may walk up and down the halls, but not on any of the other hospital floors."

Which is why they, sitting in wheelchairs,

dressed in their hospital nightgowns and matching old-lady house slippers that Millard had bought for them, ended up riding up and down in one of the elevators for an hour and a half that night. "You ready for tomorrow?" asked Sugar between floors.

"I'm a little scared. How about you?" said Tiny.

"The same."

"In case something happens . . . you know . . . tomorrow," said Tiny, "I want you to understand that I don't know what I would have done without you all of these years. Even before any of this kidney stuff came up, well, you were the best kind of friend that a person could ever hope to have."

"What?" Sugar pretended shock. "You mean I didn't have to give you my kidney for you to consider me a good friend? Shoot! I suppose that now it's too late to back out."

Just then, the elevator stopped and the doors opened up to the hospital lobby. A toothless old man in a blue bathrobe got on. He was eating Twinkies from the vending machine. "Excuse me," the man said to Sugar, holding his wrist near to her face, "but can you read what this bracelet says that they put on my arm? I left my glasses at home, and for the life of me I can't tell what it says."

"Sure," Sugar said. "Turn your wrist over so I can see. Hmm. N–P–O."

"What's that mean?" He brushed a crumb from his mouth.

Sugar looked at Tiny. She was trying not to bust with laughter. "Sir," said Sugar, "I think it means that you best not let the nurses see you eating those Twinkies."

"Oh! I remember now. When that little nurse put this thing on me, she told me I couldn't have anything else to eat or drink!"

"Don't worry," said Tiny, "we won't tell."

"Your secret is safe with us," agreed Sugar.

When, back in their rooms, they were chastised by harried nurses who had been searching for them, Tiny and Sugar both feigned ignorance. "You mean I wasn't supposed to leave this floor? I'm sorry, I misunderstood. I thought you only said that I wasn't to go to any other floor. I didn't. Promise. I never left the elevator. Not even once."

Right. Like nurses were born yesterday or something. Not to worry, the score came out even. A little while later, Sugar and Tiny's compassionate caregivers smilingly administered just revenge in the form of physician-prescribed laxatives designed to preoperatively clean out the most clogged of digestive tracts.

Just before drifting off into drug-induced dreamlands, Sugar and Tiny spoke via their hospital phones.

"See you tomorrow," whispered Tiny.

"I doubt it," said Sugar.

"I know. But maybe the day after."

"Yeah. Probably so."

Neither one wanted to hang up, but neither one could think of anything to say.

"Sweet dreams," said Tiny.

"You too. Good night," Sugar yawned.

"Good night."

It's been a year now since Tiny's successful transplant. For her, the operation wasn't so bad. She'd been so sick on dialysis that with a functioning kidney, she felt better than she had in a very long time.

Sugar's recovery was slower. Tiny was awake from surgery before her, out of bed before her, and traipsing up and down the halls before her. An unexpected infection forced Sugar, after she'd been home a week, to go back to the hospital and spend a couple of days hooked up to IVs. Even though the infection cleared up and she was back on her feet within a few weeks, she didn't get her energy back until a good six months after the surgery. During those months, Millard worried over her and daughter Shonda cooked and cleaned for her.

Tiny called her every day.

Eight months after the surgery, on the night of her birthday, Millard and Sugar lay in the dark, holding hands. "It scared me when I saw you right after the operation—all those tubes and things and them trying to get you to wake up. I was worried that you might die. Then when you got that infection . . . Sugar, I'm not ashamed to say that at the time, I was wishing with all my heart that you hadn't done this thing."

"I know," Sugar said. "It's been hard. But I'm fine now."

"Did you ever regret it?"

"No. Not really. But when the pain was so bad, I wished that I hadn't had to do it."

"Honey, was it worth it?"

"Yes. Of course. And I'll tell you exactly when I knew."

"When?"

"It was when Tiny told me that she wasn't craving sweets anymore."

"Get out of here!" Millard laughed. "Really?"

"Really. See Millard, all Tiny needed was a little pinch of Sugar. That's what I gave her, and when I see her now—all pink and prissy—I'm just so, so glad that a pinch was enough."

14

Sweet Georgia

"Dad's here! Josh—hurry up! He's here!" twelve-year-old Kevin yelled up the stairs to his twin brother before running out the door.

Josh, duffel bag in hand, bounded down the stairs, taking them two, then three at a time.

"Hey, there. Slow down," said his mother, Sarah. She was standing at the foot of the staircase, between him and his intended route of exit. "Got your toothbrush?"

"Mom! Dad's here!"

"How about your library book?"

Josh ducked around his mother. In a flash, he ran the length of the sidewalk and flew into the arms of his father, whose truck was parked on the street. "Dad!"

"Hey, guys! How you been?" He hugged and kissed them, then rubbed their heads and punched them in the arms. The boys loved it. When their mother attempted physical affection with them, however, especially outside or in public, they squirmed away, sometimes even wiped her kisses off.

Sarah, still inside the doorway of the house, felt four-footed Georgia swish past her knees. Tail wagging with the pleasure she got every time she saw Doyle, her old pal and Sarah's ex-husband, she too joined the welcoming melee, jumping and barking and licking Doyle's face.

"Georgia!" Sarah yelled.

"Hi, Sarah," Doyle said when he heard her voice and looked up.

"Hi, Doyle."

"Come on, Georgia." Doyle dragged the dog up the walk. If Georgia was in the yard when he left with the boys, in spite of the fact that she was an overweight old dog, she would chase his truck until she wore herself out. She did it every time.

Sarah took hold of the dog's collar. "Thanks, Doyle. I got her."

Josh and Kevin threw their bags into the back of Doyle's truck and climbed into the cab. "Looks like they're ready. Anything I need to know before we head out?"

"Soccer practice tomorrow at 10:00. Birthday party Sunday at 6:00."

"No problem. I'll have 'em home by 5:00. Homework?"

"Not this time. Just library books."

"Good." He yelled to the boys, "You men ready? Got your toothbrushes? No? Guys! What are you thinking? Go get 'em."

"Bye, mom!" Josh and Kevin yelled as they dashed up the stairs and then down again.

"Bye, boys!"

"Thanks, Sarah. Have a good weekend."

And then they were gone.

Georgia, as she did every time the boys left with their dad, hid behind the couch and howled. Sarah leaned against the front door, inclined to do the same. In the kitchen, she popped the top off a diet Coke and dug in her purse for her keys. When Georgia heard the jingling, she raised her head and whined. "I know. Me too," said Sarah.

Georgia cocked her head to one side.

"Let's go to the clinic. You want to? Okay. Come on. In the car." Even on a Friday evening, Sarah could find something to do—charts to complete, forms to fill out, dictation to catch up on. Something to justify getting out of the house.

The boys spent every weekend with their dad. Usually Saturdays were okay, because she kept herself busy. She went shopping, or worked in her yard, or caught up on her housework. Friday nights were the tough times. She'd tried renting movies, taking hot baths, curling up with a book. Nothing relieved the melancholy that swept over her every time she stood in the doorway of her house and watched Doyle and her boys drive off together, leaving her behind.

• • •

It wasn't supposed to turn out like this. Neither one of them ever thought that it would. But by the time Sarah and Doyle got around to seeing the minister, letting him in on the fact that they were not the perfect little family that everyone thought they were, it was already too late.

High school sweethearts, they had married at nineteen. Sarah was in college, studying to be a nurse, and Doyle was in trade school, learning to be an auto mechanic. When Sarah graduated, she began working at the nursing home in Ella Louise. When Doyle finished trade school, he honed his car-repairing skills by working in his uncle's garage. By their first anniversary, they had saved enough money to make a down payment on a double-wide trailer, which they planted on a pretty little piece of land given to them by Doyle's dad.

Josh and Kevin, twins born on Sarah and Doyle's fourth anniversary, were two weeks old when twenty-three-year-old Sarah learned of her unexpected acceptance into medical school. When she opened the acceptance letter, which Doyle had thought was a bill, she screamed so loudly that he was sure something was terribly wrong.

"I got in! I can't believe it! Doyle—I got in!"

Doyle couldn't believe it either. Though he knew that Sarah had worked for months on applications, had taken some kind of big test, and had even, while pregnant, driven to Houston for some interviews, she, not wanting to get her hopes up, had totally downplayed her chances of getting in.

Her grades weren't as high as they needed to be.

She hadn't done very well on an important interview.

The school had at least a gazillion applicants for every position they needed to fill.

She'd convinced Doyle, and herself too, that she was applying only on a whim. So remote was the possibility of acceptance that not once had Doyle and Sarah talked about what would happen if she did get accepted.

But now? Two little babies? Medical school three hours away? Doyle was proud of Sarah and all, but he didn't see how they could make it work.

Besides, he thought she liked being a nurse.

But . . . but . . . didn't he understand? This was the opportunity of a lifetime, the fulfillment of a dream! What was he saying? Sarah didn't see how they *couldn't* make it work.

Yes, she realized that Doyle had just about managed to establish himself in town as a mechanic who could be counted on to fix a person's car right. And yes, she knew that he had just bought his own little garage, where he'd hung up a sign that said "Strickland and Sons Automotive Repair." And no, she hadn't forgotten that he was *this close* to procuring a contract to maintain all of Ella Louise's school buses, fire trucks, and police cars.

Sarah and Doyle talked about medical school every night for a week. "It would mean a better life for all of us," said Sarah.

"What's wrong with the one we've got now?" said Doyle.

"Nothing. I just mean that if I were a doctor, we wouldn't have to worry so much about bills and stuff."

"You worry that much?"

"No." Sarah was quiet for a moment. "It's really not about money. I've always wanted to do more than what a nurse can do. I want to understand what's wrong with the patients I treat and why some of them get better and some of them don't. I want to be able to help in more ways than I can as a nurse. I started wanting to be a doctor when I was a little girl. My parents convinced me that being a nurse would be almost the same thing. But it's not. Doyle, I'm not that smart. I never thought I'd get in. It's an opportunity that I never dreamed I would have. And it's something I really, really want to do."

When she put it that way, there wasn't much left for Doyle to say. Who was he to say no to Sarah's dreams? He loved her and had since he was sixteen. She was right. They—rather, *he*—would find a way to make it work.

"How long will it take? All of it?" asked Doyle.

"Six years. Maybe seven."

The next day, Doyle started telling folks around town that his new business, Strickland and Sons, was up for sale.

"Any bites?" asked his neighbor.

"No."

"Sold it yet?" asked his dad.

"No."

"Don't worry. Only been a week, hasn't it, son?"

What Doyle didn't say was that when he took down his sign that said "Strickland and Sons," well, he felt like he had already sold out.

Within six months, Sarah and Doyle left Ella Louise, the town where they had both grown up, and moved into a Houston apartment close to the university.

It took not six, not seven, but eight years for Sarah to complete medical school, residency, and her internship. During those years, Doyle worked for the automotive department at Sears so they would have benefits like medical and dental insurance. He wore a uniform with his name on it. Every day he did the same three things: oil changes, brake checks, and the installation of new tires.

When he had been working at Sears for two

years, Doyle was offered the assistant manager position, but he had to turn it down. Taking the position meant working evenings and some nights, but someone had to pick up the boys from day care, and since Sarah had to be on call sometimes four or five days at a time, Doyle was that someone. He was also the someone who fixed the boys' dinners and gave them their baths.

Sarah knew that her going to school and being gone from home so much of the time was difficult on Doyle. She realized that it was not a good thing for her marriage. All she had to do was look around. A big percentage of Sarah's classmates who were married had gotten divorced along the way.

But she and Doyle were different, and so Sarah remained focused on her goal and the end that was in sight. Soon, very soon, she promised Doyle when they lay together on the nights she was home, it would be over. They would have a normal life, a better one. She would open up a practice in Ella Louise. He could buy himself another garage. They would find themselves a house. It would be good. If he, they, could just hang on.

And he told her that he could.

The May after Josh and Kevin turned eight years old, Sarah finally finished school and Doyle quit his job at Sears. Ella Louise's only physician had been wanting to retire for a couple of years. He and Sarah worked out a smooth transfer of the Family Medical Clinic as soon as she and Doyle and the boys got settled in.

For a while, all went well. Josh and Kevin, second graders by then, loved their teachers and their school.

Doyle went to work in his uncle's garage, and while his uncle wasn't ready to retire, he wanted to take time off for grandkids and fishing. Once Doyle proved that he hadn't lost his car-repairing skills, his uncle took to taking long weekends and leaving him in charge. He and Doyle began talking of Doyle leasing the place with an option to buy.

Doyle and Sarah found and bought a house. Even though they were deeply in debt, with huge student loans and credit cards charged to the max, Doyle and Sarah, lacking extravagant tastes, lived comfortably without any problem.

So what was the trouble?

What led to their separation and eventual divorce? Why, less than two years after moving back to Ella Louise, did a family such as theirs end up rent in two?

Sarah still isn't sure.

It wasn't like anybody got mad.

No one slammed any doors.

No one drove off in a huff.

No one fooled around with anybody else on the side.

But they each found themselves living in a lonely, lonely house.

"Surely you can work it out," insisted Sarah's mother. "After all you've been through? Why now?"

"Son, do you want these boys raised up in a broken home?" said Doyle's dad.

"Doyle, Sarah, God hates divorce," said their minister.

But it didn't work anymore. For either of them. And divorce seemed the logical thing to do—the rational choice for two people who had grown apart, who had nothing to say to each other, who lay beside each other night after night, careful not to touch.

Doyle and Sarah decided that they would keep it all very civil. Simple. Neither one of them would make it difficult on the other. To make the divorce easy on the boys, she would have them during the week and he would take them on the weekends.

Easy.

And so it had been for the past two years.

When Sarah was ready to leave the clinic, she turned off the lights, locked the back door, got into her car, and drove toward home. She was halfway there before she remembered that Georgia had come with her but was not in the car. Georgia? No! How could she have forgotten?

That was odd. How had she managed to get out the door without Georgia?

When Sarah got back to the clinic, she expected to see Georgia's little black nose pressed up against the clear glass door—but she didn't. Sarah entered the clinic. "Georgia," she called as she flipped on the lights. "Here, girl!"

No Georgia.

"Georgia, where are you? Are you sleeping somewhere?" The clinic wasn't that big. Sarah checked both exam rooms, the reception area, and the back office.

No Georgia.

Not in the car. Not in the clinic. Where could she be? Then Sarah remembered that after she'd been at the clinic for half an hour, she'd gone out to the car for the bottle of water and package of crackers that she always kept there. She'd propped the door to the clinic open, rather than taking the time to disengage the inside lock.

Georgia must have gotten out then.

Sarah drove home slowly, her eyes peeled for Georgia as she steered. Where would she have gone? Granted, Ella Louise wasn't that big, but neither was Georgia, and her eyes weren't as good as they used to be. Would she have headed home? Would she have been able to find her way? It was late by now. Past 10:00. Sarah drove around a couple of blocks, her eyes scanning the sides of the street. *Please God,* she prayed, *don't let her have been hit by a car. Please, please, let her be at home when I get there.*

But she wasn't. Not in the driveway. Not in the yard. Not on the porch. Sarah picked up the phone.

"Doyle, this is Sarah. Uh, I hate to ask, but has Georgia showed up over there? Well, you see, I went up to the clinic for a minute, uh, for a while, and I took her with me and somehow she slipped out when I wasn't looking. No. I'm at home. Okay. Could you call me after you take a look around? Thanks, Doyle. I'll be waiting here by the phone. No. Yes. I'm okay."

After she hung up, Sarah could do nothing but pace. Her boys loved that dog. Shoot, she was attached to Georgia too. How could she have been so careless? She tried to think. If Georgia wasn't at Doyle's, then what should she do? Stay at home and wait for her or cruise the streets looking and calling?

Why was Doyle taking so long to call back?

Then Kevin and Josh burst through the front door. "Mom! What happened to Georgia?"

"Guys—how did you get over here? Where's your dad?"

"I'm right here." Doyle was behind them. "Georgia didn't show up at my house. The boys wanted to come here. She's still not back?"

"No. Boys, I'm so sorry. I left the door propped

open while I went out to the car. She must have slipped out then."

"Dad, what should we do?" asked Kevin.

"Georgia's never tried to run away before," said Josh.

"Let's get in the truck and drive around and look for her," said Doyle. "You want to come, Sarah?"

All four of them piled into the cab of the truck, and Doyle slowly drove the streets of Ella Louise. Every so often he stopped and the four of them got out. "Georgia! Georgia! Here, girl. Here, Georgia," they called.

No Georgia. After an hour, Doyle turned the truck toward Sarah's house. What else was there to do? The boys were silent, but Sarah could feel their accusatory thoughts. She wondered if Doyle was accusing her too.

But when Doyle pulled the truck into the driveway, there was Georgia, illuminated by the headlights of the truck, wagging her tail. The boys tumbled out of the car.

"Georgia!"

She sprang into their arms.

"You were a bad dog!"

She wriggled with delight.

"We looked everywhere for you!"

She licked one boy's face, then the other's. Then she bounded over to where Doyle and Sarah stood, ran around them both, and went back again to the boys.

Sarah turned to Doyle. "I don't know where she was or how she got home, but it feels good to know that I won't be the one sleeping in the doghouse tonight."

Doyle grinned. "It wasn't your fault."

"Right. Tell that to those two," she said, motioning to the boys. "You know, they're not going to be ready to go for a while. Want some coffee?"

"Sure."

Sarah and Doyle sat at the kitchen table while Josh and Kevin romped with Georgia in the family room. "Guys. Settle down," Sarah called to them. "Don't wear that poor dog out. Did anybody feed her? Josh, is that one of your good socks that Georgia's got in her mouth?"

"No, Mom," said Josh.

"It's one of yours," teased Kevin.

"House looks good," said Doyle.

"Thanks."

"How's work?"

"Good. Yours?"

"Going good."

The family room became quiet. Sarah looked in on the boys. The two of them, with Georgia between, lay side by side on the floor, watching a video that Kevin had put in. Georgia, when she heard Sarah, got up, stretched, and yawned. She followed Sarah back to the kitchen.

"Hey, girl," Doyle said when he saw the dog. "Big night?"

Georgia rested her head on his knee.

"She misses you," Sarah said.

"Yeah. I miss her too. Old Georgia here is a good ole dog," Doyle said.

Sarah took a sip of coffee.

"Remember when we got her?" he asked.

"Sure do. Same day that we found out that the twins were coming. You surprised me with her—" she began.

"And you surprised me with them," finished Doyle. Neither one of them spoke for a minute, then suddenly Sarah was blindsided by sobs that she was powerless to stop. Embarrassed, she covered her face with her hands. "I'm sorry." Her shoulders shook with her efforts to stop.

Doyle reached into his back pocket and pulled out a red hankie. "It's okay. Here."

"Thanks." Deep breaths. Breathe in. Breathe out. Sarah blew her nose and wiped her eyes, but as soon as she did that, she started up again. She had not cried in front of Doyle in many years.

"It's all right," he said.

"No. I don't want the boys to hear."

Doyle got up to get her water, but he couldn't find the glasses. Sarah tried to direct him. "To the right. Up. Over. No, down." He opened cabinet doors left and right.

Sarah laughed. "Thank you," she said when he finally brought her the drink.

"You're welcome."

"Doyle, do you hate this as much as I do?"

"Yeah."

"How did we let this happen?"

"I don't know."

"Georgia's not the only one around here who misses you. It's all I can do every Friday when she tries to chase your truck, not to let loose of her collar and chase you too."

"Really?"

"Really. . . . Is it too late—for us, I mean?"

"Way I always figured it," said Doyle, "it wouldn't be too late until one of us got married to someone else."

"You engaged?" Sarah asked.

"No."

"Me neither."

"Listen," said Doyle. "Hear that? Snoring. Boys are asleep."

"Why don't you stay in the extra room," said Sarah. "No need to wake them up. I'll fix us all breakfast in the morning."

"You sure?"

"Yes, I'm sure."

And later that night when Georgia jumped up on the foot of his bed, Doyle was grateful to get the chance to sleep with at least one of the girls that he loved.

● ● ●

For the past six months, neither Sarah nor Georgia have had to fight the urge to chase Doyle's truck on Friday nights. They're still on their own when it comes to filling their Saturdays, but every Friday evening, at Doyle's invitation, Sarah and Georgia pile into the truck with Kevin and Josh and go to Doyle's house for conversation, fun, and food. They have a great time. Sarah looks forward to it all week.

It's too soon to tell if Doyle and Sarah will get back together. They still have a lot of things they need to talk about—hurts, resentments, misunderstandings that won't go away by themselves. It simply won't do to smooth over such things and pretend that everything is all right.

Doyle knows that. Sarah knows that. They're taking things slowly.

But in her heart, Sarah believes that Friday nights are a start.

And Georgia, sweet Georgia, is inclined to agree.

15

Old Spice

Rocky Shartle believes in love at first sight. Of course he does. His bride of four years, Rochelle, stole his heart the first time he laid eyes on her. Their meeting was terribly romantic, Rocky believes.

More like terribly painful, Rochelle contends. She's got the scars to prove it.

Even though he and Rochelle have been married for four years and share their home with two rowdy little kids, Rocky, a gentle and sentimental man, gets misty-eyed and runny-nosed when he talks about it.

The two of them were living in Houston when they met. Twenty-year-old Rocky was a student at the local university. He was an education major, and before doing his student teaching he was required to complete twenty hours of observation inside a public-school classroom. Not being very outgoing or brave about doing new things, Rocky's hands were sweaty on his car's steering wheel on the first morning that he arrived at the school. He didn't know any of the teachers, the administration, or any of the students. He wasn't sure what to expect or even what was expected of him. And where was he supposed to go? Rocky looked around. The campus was large, with several official-looking buildings. His advisor had told him to arrive early and check in at the office. The main door, the one he should go in, would be unlocked.

But there were a lot of doors to the inside. Which one was which? What if he accidentally set off some kind of alarm or something?

Rocky was sitting in his car, contemplating what to do next, when he spotted seventeen-year-old Rochelle. She was hard to miss, as she was perched six feet above the ground on a two-by-two foot metal platform in the middle of a blocked-off portion of the student parking lot. Both her red hair and her short skirt flying and flipping in the wind drew Rocky's gaze. At first he wondered what she was doing up there—it looked to him like she was reading something from a book. But when he saw sleepy-eyed students stagger from the building, carrying horns and drums, he figured it out. Of course. The red-haired girl was the drum major. Marching band practice was about to commence.

Since the band's rehearsal hadn't yet started, Rocky decided to ask the red-haired girl for directions. He grabbed his book satchel, got out of his car, and strode to the girl's perch. "Excuse me?" Rocky stood on the ground and looked up. "Could you tell me where I . . . oh!"

Rochelle had been so intent on looking over her music score, on making sure that she understood all the changes that the band director had asked her to make in the band's routine, that she hadn't heard Rocky come up. When he spoke, his voice startled her and she jumped, stumbled backwards in what seemed like slow motion, and tumbled right off the platform, landing in a twisted heap.

Band members who saw what had happened rushed to Rochelle's aid. One of them ran to tell the band director that he better come quick. Rocky, mortified that he'd caused Rochelle to fall, did not know what to do.

"Oh! I'm so sorry! Are you all right?"

Rochelle, stunned and in pain, tried to assure Rocky and the rest of those gathered around her that she was okay. "I'm fine. Just fine." She looked up at Rocky. "Could you help me get up? I think I may have twisted something."

Help her up? Could he ever! The sight of Rochelle's hazel-green eyes, framed with thick brown lashes and wet with tears of pain, gave the slight-built Rocky a strength he had not known before. Though she outweighed him by about ten pounds, Rocky lifted Rochelle in his arms and carried her all the way to the band hall. He only nearly dropped her twice.

"He was my knight in pressed khakis," teased Rochelle when she overheard him telling Melissa, the waitress at the Wild Flour, how they met. "I knew from then on that Rocky was the only man for me."

"You did not. You hardly knew I was alive, until you got out of school. The hard part," Rocky told Melissa, "was that I couldn't let on that I liked her or I would have gotten kicked out of the teaching program at the university. She never even knew."

"But I thought you said that you were just a student too," said Melissa. "You were only there for a couple of weeks of observation, right?"

"I was, but then I ended up doing some substitute teaching at that school—which in one way was a good thing, because I made a little money and got to see Rochelle every day, but in another way was a bad thing, because I couldn't let on that I liked her."

"They have strict rules about teachers, even substitute teachers, having anything to do with students," said Rochelle.

"So for twelve long weeks, I admired my redhead darling from afar."

"And for twelve weeks, I hobbled around in a cast."

"You mean your leg was broken?"

Rochelle pulled up her skirt a bit to show

Melissa the evidence. "Yep. Had to have surgery and everything."

"Rochelle wasn't my first girlfriend," Rocky said, "but she was the first girl that I actually caused to fall head over heels!"

Rocky knows it didn't happen exactly like that, but he thinks it makes for a good how-we-met tale. Actually, he was the one who fell for Rochelle. Hard. Though he never acted on his feelings while he was assigned to her school (so fearful was he of getting in trouble that he hardly dared speak to her), every single day his eyes sought her out. He snatched glimpses of her hobbling on her crutches down the school hallways, watched her laugh with her friends in the school cafeteria, and tried to act nonchalant when she passed by his classroom.

"Leg healing okay?" Rocky would ask about once a week.

"Okay," she said.

"That's good."

The day after Rochelle graduated from high school, Rocky called her up.

"Rocky? Rocky who? Rocky Shartle? *Mr.* Shartle? Uh, yeah, I mean, yes, sir, I mean, yes, this is Rochelle."

"Are you feeling all right? Your leg, I mean?"

"Yes. I'm totally fine. I don't even have to go back for more therapy."

"Good. I'm glad." Silence. A deep breath. "I was wondering if you would like to go out sometime. Maybe Saturday? To a movie?"

"Well, sure. I mean, I guess so."

"Great. I'll pick you up at 6:30. Would that be all right?"

"Okay, Mr. Sh—Rocky. That sounds like fun."

Well, Rocky decided that very evening, the night of their first date, that Rochelle was the woman he was going to marry. It took Rochelle a little longer. Not until their third date did she decide Rocky was right for her.

"What will your parents think when we tell them we want to get married?" he asked.

"I dunno. Actually, I think they'll be shocked, and since I'm only eighteen, they'll probably try to talk us into waiting. Then again, they can't say much. They were only eighteen themselves when they got married. Actually, once they get over the surprise, I think they'll decide it's okay. You gonna talk to my dad?"

-"I think I should."

"How about my mom?"

"Yes. Her too."

Rochelle's parents lived a thousand miles away. Because of her dad's job, they'd had to move just six weeks before her graduation. They had allowed Rochelle to stay behind and live with a friend so that she could graduate from her hometown high school. Rocky and Rochelle's marriage plans would have to be discussed over the phone.

Rocky fortified himself with three swigs of Pepto-Bismol before gathering the courage to call Rochelle's dad and ask him for his daughter's hand.

"Hi, Daddy," Rochelle said after she'd dialed the phone. "How are you? I'm fine. Yes. Yes. Okay. I sure will. Uh, Daddy, remember the guy that I told you about? Uh-huh, that's the one. Rocky, the one who's going to be a teacher. Well, he's here with me now and he wants to ask you something."

"Mr. Riggs," Rocky said, his voice sounding high inside his own head, "Rochelle and I would like to get married, if that's all right with you, uh, sir."

Rochelle, only inches away, tried to read Rocky's face and guess her daddy's response.

"Yes. Yes. In May, after I graduate, sir. Uh, no, sir, but I have several leads. Uh-huh, I mean, yes, sir. Of course. Yes. I promise. You have my word on that. Yes. Okay. Good-bye, sir. Thank you. Thank you very much."

He laid the phone back into its cradle and sank to a chair, sweating and grinning and thinking that he might throw up.

"Well? What did he say? Did he say okay? Did he sound upset? Tell me!" Rochelle hopped from one foot to the other.

"He said we could get married as long as I promised to . . ." Rochelle's dad's words suddenly registered in Rocky's brain, "take care of your teeth?"

Just then the phone rang. It was Rochelle's mother. Her dad had hung up before she'd had a chance to talk, and that was not all right by her. "Yes, mother, I'm sure. I know, but we don't want to wait. Oh yes, he's very good to me. You do? All right, I'll put him on."

Rochelle handed the phone to Rocky. He drew back from it as if it were a snake. "She wants to talk to you," Rochelle hissed.

"Yes, ma'am. Uh-huh. Yes. I understand. Yes. I'll do my best." He hung up the phone again.

"Rocky! I wanted to talk to her some more. What did she say? I couldn't tell if she was excited or upset. How do you think she sounded?"

"Rochelle, is there something you haven't told me?"

"What do you mean? What did she say?"

"She only wanted to know one thing. If we got married, would I take care of your teeth? Your dad asked me the same thing. You don't have, like . . . are those your real teeth?" He looked at her mouth. "I mean, your teeth aren't going to fall out or something, are they?"

Rochelle began to giggle. "No. Of course not. It's just that when I was younger, when my permanent teeth first started coming in, I had lots of problems and my parents had to spend a ton of money on my mouth. And my parents are not rich. For years and years, I had to go to the dentist almost every month. It nearly worried my mother and daddy to death. But my teeth are fine now."

Rocky did not look convinced.

Rochelle opened her mouth and showed him her teeth. "See? They're fine. You're looking at a very expensive smile. I guess Mom and Dad just want to make sure that their investment is well taken care of."

Once he'd finished telling Melissa the story, Rocky looked at his watch, gave Rochelle a peck on the cheek, and left to pick the kids up from the baby-sitter. Melissa watched him go, then turned to Rochelle. "You agreed to marry Rocky on your third date? And you were only eighteen?"

"It was his cologne," said Rochelle.

"No!"

"Really. Old Spice. When I saw it in his bathroom—five full bottles—well, I just knew that Rocky was the one."

"Pee-yew! I don't like Old Spice," said Melissa. "I've never smelled it on Rocky."

And she never will. Rocky doesn't wear the stuff. But he gets a brand-new bottle every year at Christmas.

Rocky's Granny Opal, in her younger, more spry years, loved to go shopping, especially for Christmas presents. She'd never learned to drive, so in early December (Granny Opal liked to beat the crowds), her daughter-in-law, Rocky's mother, would pick her up and take her to Sears, J.C. Penney's, and Wal-Mart. Granny Opal would search for perfect gifts for her children, her grandchildren, her next-door neighbors, and the preacher at her church. The two of them, mother-in-law and daughter-in-law, enjoyed each other's company, and so they would make a day of it, stopping midmorning for coffee and midday for lunch.

Granny Opal always got Rocky's mother to help her pick out her own gift. "Promise me, though, that between now and Christmas, you'll forget what it is," she would say with a wink.

"I promise." Rocky's mother always kept her word.

In her seventy-third year, Granny Opal's legs got bad, and she found it difficult to get around. She continued to go to church once a week, but that was about all. Rocky's mother brought her groceries. His dad took her to the doctor when she needed to go.

Soon after Thanksgiving that year, Granny Opal began to fret about how she was going to manage Christmas.

"Let's not worry about it," Rocky's mother said. "There is no need for you to be getting any of us gifts this year. Being together is all the gift that we need."

But Granny Opal would hear none of that. Nothing would do but that she make out a list and that Rocky's mother go and get what was on the list. "I'm going to make it easy on you, hon," she said after giving the list some thought. "I want you to buy chocolate-covered cherries— one box for each of the neighbors and two for the preacher. And for you girls, good white slips." Granny believed that no decent woman ever left her house without a slip; some dresses might even require two. "And since I've been studying on it, I think all the boys would enjoy some Old Spice."

Rocky's mother told Granny Opal that her ideas were excellent.

So that year on Christmas morning, in front of Granny Opal's pleased face, the entire family, including sixteen-year-old Rocky, opened up their gifts.

"Thanks, Granny! I needed a new slip."

"Thank you, Granny, for the Old Spice."

The gifts went over so well that next year, Granny had Rocky's mother buy everyone the same thing.

"Thank you, Granny!"

"Thanks, Granny!"

And so it went the next year and the next. After the fourth year of Old Spice and new slips, Rocky's mother came up with a plan. Since none of the guys actually wore the Old Spice, and since a woman can really only use so many slips, she decided that this year everyone should put their gifts in a big box. She would then store the gifts and when Granny Opal told her to go shopping the next year, she would simply take them out of storage and wrap them up again. Granny didn't need to know. She would still get the pleasure of seeing them open up their gifts, but there would be less waste.

What a great idea! Everyone agreed.

Everyone except for nineteen-year-old Rocky. He loved Granny Opal, and it just didn't seem right to fool her like that. No one meant any disrespect to Granny, but he did not see it that way. No, he didn't wear Old Spice. But no, he wasn't going to give it back. Granny had given it to him, and he wanted to keep it.

And so he did.

"Melissa, when I saw that Rocky had almost half a dozen bottles of Old Spice in his bathroom cabinet, and when he told me about how his Granny Opal gave them to him every year and all of the rest, well, I fell in love. My Rocky is a sweet, sweet man."

"You're right. He is a good man," Melissa said. "Is Granny Opal still alive?"

"Nope. She passed away the January after he and I got married. But you know, every year under the tree at our house, Rocky still finds a bottle of—"

"Old Spice?"

"Yep. I take one of those bottles down out of the cabinet, wrap it up, and tell him it's from Granny Opal. He always says it's his favorite gift."

A sweet man with a stockpile of stuff to make him smell even sweeter. What more could a gal ask for in a man? Nothing—not one thing—if his wife, Rochelle, is at all to be believed.

Personally, I think she is.

16

All the Right Ingredients

It was Alfred Tinker who came up with the idea of holding the first annual Ella Louise Gumbo Cook-off. Since his wife, Tiny, whose opinion he valued, thought the idea a good one, he brought it up to the Saturday morning coffee drinkers gathered at the Wild Flour Café.

Crow Buxley scratched his head. "Mayor, we've already got the May Okra Fest. Lots of cooking goes on then. You wanting to add something to that?"

"No, no. I'm talking about a separate event altogether. Not connected to the Okra Fest."

"When you thinking about having it?" asked Rocky Shartle.

"First weekend in November. It'll be cold enough so we won't have to worry about any of the fixings going bad, but early enough so bad weather shouldn't be much of a concern," said the mayor. "I'm thinking we'd hold it at the park. Have everybody do their cooking over camp-fires. Maybe invite some of those Cajun boys up from Louisiana to play us some tunes."

"Sounds like a good idea to me," said Doyle Strickland.

"Everybody 'round here likes gumbo. Something like that ought to draw a good crowd," said Rocky.

"I say we need some kind of community event in the fall," said Doyle. "Not much going on once high school football's over."

"That's what I'm thinking," said the mayor. "The event could be a moneymaker too. Once the judging's been done, we could sell the gumbo by the bowl or by the quart for folks who want to take some home. I figure we'd charge enough to cover our costs plus a little. Whatever extra we make, we can donate to the city council college scholarship fund."

"You planning on giving out prizes?" asked Rocky.

"To get folks to enter, I imagine we'll need to. First place, second place, third, and honorable mention. Trophies, probably. Maybe some cash or a gift certificate. Which do you think?"

Trophies. Crow and Rocky and the rest of the boys agreed.

"Whole thing'd be more festive if you asked folks to decorate their campsite," said Chief Johnson.

"You could give a prize for the best one," said Rocky.

The mayor stood to go. "Thanks, men. You've

been a big help. I believe come Monday, Faye Beth and I will start putting the thing together."

Faye Beth agreed that the cook-off idea was a good one. "How about a dessert contest too? That and a craft show would be fun. And say, a square dance that night, wouldn't that be festive? Maybe a petting zoo for the kids?" Her eyes shone as she got excited.

Elected in part because of his diplomacy, Mayor Tinker gently disagreed. "Faye Beth, those are fine ideas, but we don't want to take away from the Okra Fest. And, you know, I'm not crazy about the idea of having a petting zoo anywhere near where there's food being cooked. Kids these days don't wash their hands like they should. I say we just stick with gumbo and a little music. See how it goes. We can always add to the event next year."

"Of course. You're right. I just get carried away," agreed Faye Beth. "But Mayor, folks are going to expect some dessert. You think a bake sale would be too much?"

"Why, no," he conceded. "I think a sale without a contest would be fine. You want to let all the church ladies know?"

She would.

By the end of the day, a date for the first annual Ella Louise Gumbo Cook-off had been set—the first Saturday in November. By the end of the week, Mayor Tinker had recruited a panel of judges, the identities of whom Faye Beth thought should be kept anonymous until the day of the contest.

Mayor Tinker agreed.

At the suggestion of the judges, cook-off rules were drafted. Advised by the home economist at the county Farm Extension Office, and after much discussion, Faye Beth and Mayor Tinker narrowed the list down to five rules.

1. Only in-date, store-bought, USDA-inspected meat, seafood, or poultry products may be used. No squirrel, opossum, or dove meat allowed. No Exceptions!!!
2. There is no official gumbo recipe. However, in keeping with Ella Louise's status as the self-proclaimed okra capital of Texas, contestants should be advised that the official judges will look closely at the okra content of each recipe when determining the winner.
3. No tobacco use within three feet of the cooking pots. (Yes, this includes snuff and chewing tobacco.)
4. Cooks are required to wear aprons and hats.
5. All gumbo is to be prepared in cast-iron pots provided by the city of Ella Louise. Pots and cooking stands will be delivered to each campsite by 6:00 A.M. on the morning of the cook-off.

With the procurement of borrowed pots and stands from the nearby town of Pearly, which held a chili cook-off every year, and with a funeral-home awning to shield the baked goods from the weather, Faye Beth believed they had all the bases covered.

Within a week of announcing the cook-off, via posters placed at Tawny's Quick Tan, the library, the grocery store, Lindell's Clean-It-Quick Car Wash, and the Wild Flour Café, Mayor Tinker had received and Faye Beth had validated twelve gumbo-cooking teams, six from Ella Louise and six from out of town.

Of the thirty-dollar registration checks received, only Crow Buxley's bounced.

"You want me to call him?" asked Faye Beth.

"No. Don't embarrass the man," said the mayor. "Crow never has been very good at math. He probably got mixed up as to what day the government deposits his check. What's today? The second? Send it back through. It should clear if it hits the bank today."

He was right. Crow's check cleared just fine the second time around.

Folks all over town were excited. The ladies of the various Ella Louise churches planned to sell pies and cakes by the slice. Chief Johnson decided to cook some of his Indian fry bread and give it away for free.

"It being the same month as Thanksgiving, I

thought it only fitting. Besides, fry bread will be good with gumbo. Mayor, what are you doing about rice?"

Mayor Tinker hadn't thought of that. There had to be rice. He scratched his head. Who could he talk into cooking up a pot? He phoned Bessie Bishop, this year's president of the Gentle Thimble Quilting Club.

Sure. The Gentle Thimbles would be happy to be in charge of rice. She would drive over to Sam's Club and pick up a big bag. She needed to go anyway. Would fifty pounds be enough?

"Lands, yes," said the mayor. "More than. You ladies don't know how much I appreciate it. And yes, of course the club may set up a card table to raffle off a quilt."

"Mayor," asked Faye Beth two days before the big day, "have you called the portable toilet people?"

"Shoot. I knew I forgot something. Can you get 'em on the phone? Faye Beth, how many do you think we'll need?"

Details, details. Mayor Tinker hoped he had remembered everything.

Meanwhile, the Ella Louise folks who were planning on entering the contest began their preparations in earnest.

Ten days before the cook-off, members of the Family Medical Clinic staff team, made up of

Dr. Sarah Strickland, nurse Janet Evans, and receptionist Esther Vaughn, shared a sack of microwave popcorn during their midmorning break and discussed their proposed entry into the contest. Only problem was that halfway through the bag of popcorn they found themselves in a heated disagreement as to how best prepare their gumbo's roux—the cooked mixture of flour and fat essential to the making of all gumbos.

"My granny never used anything but bacon grease, and she was born and raised in Louisiana," Janet said.

"No, Crisco works best," said Esther. "Makes a smoother, more consistent roux. Browns up better and there's less worry about scorching."

Sarah pulled rank. "Uh-uh. Bacon grease and Crisco are both saturated fats—bad for the heart. We need to set a healthy example by using liquid corn oil. Nothing else. There's enough heart disease in this county. I'm not going to be accused of adding to my business by clogging up folks' arteries more than they already are. And as for the flour—"

"Not whole wheat," pleaded Janet.

"Please?" said Esther.

"Nothing but," said Sarah.

Esther and Janet's heads both dropped. Their chances of winning had just sunk to nil.

Todd and Patricia Scutter, who since the adoption of their darling Honduran daughter had been fascinated by anything remotely related to Latin America, planned to prepare their gumbo with a south-of-the-border flair. Chopped chilies, fresh cilantro, and copious amounts of ground cumin were what they planned to use in seasoning their pot.

Patricia looked forward to her and the baby wearing the fancy embroidered dresses she had bought on the adoption trip she and Todd had made to Honduras. Todd, though slightly less enthused, agreed to don a serape for the day. To set a festive scene, they decided to decorate their cooking site with multicolored lights and piñatas hung from the trees.

When contestant Tim Hartford, who had been living with Rocky and Rochelle Shartle for the past few months, told everyone at the Wild Flour about his plan to cook up a vegetarian gumbo, folks coughed, shuffled their feet, and avoided his gaze. No one wanted to be rude. By all accounts, Tim seemed to be as nice a young man as could be. Of course, being from New Jersey, he couldn't be expected to know that any gumbo fit to be consumed by true-blue, God-fearing Americans would contain at least three, possibly four or even five varieties of animal products.

As for Tim's plan to decorate his cooking site with a Hawaiian theme—palm trees, crepe-paper leis, and tiki torches—well, folks around Ella Louise had never heard of such a thing.

Bessie Bishop, because of her tasty contributions to several church potlucks, had established herself as a good cook. However, when turning in her entry form, she let it slip that she had never in her life made gumbo. Folks in the know immediately counted her out. One did not come to gumbo-cooking overnight.

Bessie didn't see how cooking gumbo could be that hard, especially considering the fact that she was once a finalist in the Pillsbury regional bake-off. She searched the Internet for the perfect recipes. She firmly believed that the key to preparing a winning dish—whether it be apple pie or fig preserves, or gumbo, for that matter—was to use the freshest ingredients possible. Before moving to Ella Louise, Bessie had lived in Houston, and she had a few secret seafood-supplier tricks up her sleeve. Not only that, in the little greenhouse behind her home, Bessie was growing tomatoes, okra, green onions, and four different kinds of peppers. Those just-plucked veggies would be her ticket to first prize. She was sure of it.

Truth was, Polly Ann and Molly Jan Pierce were looked upon by most everyone in Ella Louise as the team most likely to take first prize. And no wonder. The sisters had an outstanding culinary reputation. Every year, the two of them dominated at least three out of seven categories of the cooking contest held during Ella Louise's annual Okra Festival.

The ladies had a way with food.

Rumor had it that their entry would be concocted from an old family recipe, a secret one handed down from their great-great-granddaddy on their mother's side, who was known to be an outstanding river-barge cook. Unlike many of their peers, Polly and Molly believed in the exact measuring of every ingredient. If their great-great-granddaddy's gumbo was good, well, it was assumed that the sisters' would be exactly the same.

Because he didn't get page two of the rules, contestant Crow Buxley did not know that cooking pots would be provided for cook-off contestants. He thought that he had to provide his own. So a big part of his preparation for the cook-off was to make a trip to the nearest hardware store, located in Pearly, a good thirty-minute drive from Ella Louise.

The price of the pot and rack gave him a start. Sure sounded high. Then he thought better of it. The pot would be something good to have on hand. He could use it for stew, chili, even for minestrone soup, should he care to cook for a big outside crowd some time. Why, next time there was a family reunion, he could take his pot and feed the whole clan something good.

"You do know, Mr. Buxley, that you'll need to season your pot before you use it the first time," said the woman when he hefted the thing up onto the counter to check out.

"No. Don't reckon I do," said Crow.

"If you don't, everything you cook in it will stick and burn."

Sticking? Burning? That wouldn't do.

"It's easy. All you do is rub oil all over it. Take the racks out of your oven at home and then put that pot, lid and all, inside. Turn on your oven to about four hundred degrees. Leave it in there a good hour or so. Once the pot cools down, it wouldn't hurt to repeat the process another couple of times. You can't season a pot like this too much. The more you do it, the better it'll cook. Will this be all for you today?"

Crow thought a minute. Seemed like there was something else.

"Bug spray. Wasp and hornet. A whole mess of wasps are bent on building their nests under the eaves of my house."

"How many cans you need?" she asked.

"Two ought to be enough," said Crow. "Thank you. Honey, there's no need to put 'em in a sack." He lifted the lid of the pot. "Just set 'em in here. Yes. That'll be fine. Now, how much is it that I owe you?"

Crow waited until the Friday evening before the Saturday contest to season his pot. He figured that way the pot would be fresh. Everything else was all in order. Crow's gumbo recipe called for shrimp, crab, crawfish, sausage, and chicken, and he had all of them already cleaned and prepared. Crow also had his tomatoes and celery and onions all chopped up and secured into individual twist-tie-closed bread bags. His seasonings were measured out, but in case he hadn't figured right, he planned to take the individual containers with him as well. Most important of all, Crow had his flour and grease in coffee cans so as to be ready to make up his roux.

Now. To season the pot. Wonder why they called it seasoning? Didn't the woman say all you had to do was rub oil on it and heat it up real hot? Crow hoisted the pot onto the counter in his kitchen. He turned on the oven, then remembered that he needed to take the racks out for the pot to fit. By now the racks were hot. Not wanting to burn his countertop or the floor, Crow put the racks on the back porch.

So.

Now.

Oil.

How to put the oil on? Crow decided that a sponge would work for the task. Sure enough, the sponge did an excellent job. Carefully, Crow rubbed oil over the sides of the pot, underneath the bottom, even on the little feet. He didn't forget to oil the top or the handle either, though he wasn't sure doing so was necessary. The pot looked good with its shiny coat of oil. Once he was done, Crow heaved the pot into the oven, closed the door, and went into the living room to rest. All that cooking and chopping and peeling and oiling had pretty much worn him out.

Crow guessed that he must have dozed off, because the next thing he knew, the phone was ringing.

"Hello."

"Crow. It's me. Bessie. You all ready for tomorrow?"

"Just about. Got my pot in the oven."

"What pot?" asked Bessie.

"My gumbo pot. Got it in the oven. Seasoning. So nothing will stick," he said.

"But Crow, the city's providing pots. You don't have to bring your—" Bessie's sentence was interrupted by a roof-raising sound.

Ca-boom. CA-BOOM! CRASH!!!

"Crow!" she cried.

She heard his phone drop.

"Crow! Crow!"

What in the world could that crashing sound have been? She had to go see. In her haste, she couldn't find her car keys. Rats! Where were they? After a few minutes of searching, Bessie gave up, put on a sweater over her purple lounging pajamas, and set out in a trot. It was a quarter mile to Crow's house.

The headlights of Mayor Tinker's car fell on Bessie as she hurried along on the side of the street. He rolled down his window.

"Bessie? That you? What are you doing walking at this time of evening?"

She was out of breath and obviously upset. "It's Crow," she huffed. "Something's wrong. I don't know what. We were talking. There was this big bang. He dropped the phone."

Mayor Tinker reached over and opened the passenger door for her to get in. When they arrived at Crow's house, his front door was unlocked.

"Crow," called the mayor, who went in first, "you all right?"

"Crow?" called Bessie.

There was a terrible smell in the house. They went on in and found Crow in the kitchen, standing, dizzy and dazed in front of his stove. What once had been an oven door was now a black, smoking hole. The door had been blown clean off its hinges and had landed across the room, where it now lay melting the vinyl floor. Also of note were the remains of a couple of cans of wasp and hornet spray that could be seen in other parts of the room.

As for the stove?

Dead, all of its wiring fried to a crisp.

"Crow! My word! What happened here?" said Bessie. "You could have been killed!"

She was so glad that he hadn't been.

I recently attended the fifth annual Ella Louise Gumbo Cook-off. It's an event that I try never to miss. I know that while I'm there, I'll get to see old friends, catch up on the local gossip and goings on in the town, and always, always hear the tale of how Crow Buxley, preparing to make gumbo, nearly blew up his house.

Poor Crow.

He's taken a lot of ribbing over the years. Luckily, he's good-natured about it, even though the story grows bigger and funnier every time that it's told. When Crow overhears someone relating the tale to me, when he sees me nodding and pretending that it's the first time I've ever heard the story, he sneaks me a wink.

I know exactly what that wink means.

Sometime later that day, he and I will slip off somewhere by ourselves. We'll get us a couple of Dr. Peppers, find a comfortable, out-of-the-way place to sit, and have us a nice long chat.

Well out of the earshot of the others, Crow'll tell me about Molly Jan and Polly Ann Pierce's recent shopping trip to Dallas, and why they are no longer allowed to set foot inside Neiman Marcus, their all-time favorite department store.

Crow will tell me about the crazy and up-until-now covered-up incident involving the leaky baptistery over at Chosen Vessel Church and what that has to do with the stitches on the forehead of Millard Fry.

I'll learn touching details about the melancholy romance between Melissa Bates, waitress at the

Wild Flour, and Tim Hartford, the town mime. He'll tell me why folks are hoping and praying (bless those two kids' hearts) that it'll last.

Eventually, Crow and I will finish our cold drinks. I'll be the first one to look at my watch, stand up, and stretch. "Guess I best be heading toward home," I'll say.

"When you expect to be back up our way?" Crow will ask.

"Soon," I'll say. And it's the truth. In a place like Ella Louise, there are always more stories to be shared. And since tales of small-town life are among my most favorite things, I'll be back for more.

You can count on that.

Annette loves to hear from her readers. If you wish to contact her, write to

Annette Smith,
P.O. Box 213,
Grandview TX 76050

or e-mail her at author@academicplanet.com

For information about scheduling Annette to speak at your next event, contact

Speak Up Speaker Services
(888) 870-7719

or on the web at
www.speakupspeakerservices.com

Center Point Large Print
600 Brooks Road / PO Box 1
Thorndike ME 04986-0001 USA

(207) 568-3717

US & Canada:
1 800 929-9108
www.centerpointlargeprint.com

8114